I0451853

# Hitman's Honey

## A Romance Suspense Thriller

### Kay Freeman

Copyright © 2023 by Kay Klotzbach/Kay Freeman/Kay Freeman LLC

All rights reserved.

No part of this book may be reproduced in any form or by any electronic or mechanical means, including information storage and retrieval systems, without written permission from the author, except for the use of brief quotations in a book review.

For permission requests, contact: kf@kaylaafreeman.com or klotzba1@mac.com

The story, all names, characters, and incidents portrayed in this production are fictitious. No identification with actual persons (living or deceased), places, buildings, and products is intended or should be inferred.

Digital ISBN#: 979-8-9853618-0-3

Paperback ISBN#: 979-8-9853618-3-4

Published in the United States of America

# Dedication

*"This book is dedicated to all those over the age of fifty who are still getting it on. We don't have to wear our cloaks of invisibility."*

# Acknowledgments

Thank you to my editor, Jason Pettus, for all you do to make my books the best they can be.

Thank you to Romance Writers of America for offering workshops and classes and supporting romance writers.

Cover Credit: bookcoversonline.com

# Content Warning

This suspense romance novel contains **<u>Age 18+ Content</u>**. The heroine suffers from an eating disorder. The book also contains graphic descriptions of sexual activities and scenes of violence. If you find any of this objectionable or triggering, stay clear. However, with all this said, the book is healing and hopeful and ends with a positive, loving relationship.

# Chapter 1
# Love is Honey

"Life is a flower, of which love is honey."

— —Victor Hugo

 Thursday

Rylee never thought she'd die like this, in the Atlantic Ocean. It was only a week ago at the 2022 Romance Writers of America Conference in Maryland at the Gaylord Hotel when she had stood at the registration table and slipped the lanyard with her maiden name, Rylee Reed, over her head, that everything changed.

She had dreams and things she wanted to achieve, but they meant nothing now as she swallowed salty water and understood these trappings of success have little to do with what really matters in life.

Good and bad people had entered her world throughout her

life, and often Rylee couldn't tell the difference. This time, one she thought she'd loved and had loved her tried to take everything away, including her life. Her story is about how an assassin twice saved her, and you won't find it written on paper inside a bottle washed up on any beach. You'll find it here, in the words that follow these...

* * *

The Previous Thursday

He leaned his elbows on the railing, searching the horde below. "There's a right way and a wrong way to do things, Connie," he remembered Pally saying. *Can I do this the right way?* The unfortunate thing was, if he did, his target Lyndon Roach the Third, Vice President of Truth Systems Inc., would be history by tomorrow, and he would have to return home. The upside—Connor could watch his favorite soccer team, Galway United, play this weekend.

Connor loved hotels like this. The Gaylord, outside of Washington, D.C., was Disneyland for adults. Everything was self-contained: restaurants, bars, cafes, sleeping quarters, exercise areas and shops under one roof. Plus, Connor didn't stand out. He was just one of thousands of attendees here for a conference. Of course, Connor was an expert at blending in. It had become even easier since he'd gotten older. People seemed to ignore older blokes; somehow, he'd traded in his good looks for a cloak of invisibility when he'd turned fifty.

Connor walked to the escalator that carried him down to the lobby and tailed his mark into the cafe. An enormous blackboard listed all the possibilities for coffee and tea drinks. The varieties here were endless: cafe latte, Americano, cafe mocha, cortado, espresso, cappuccino, it just went on and on. And the dozens of syrups extended the flavor experience further. And that was just the coffee menu. Connor remembered when you had two choices: coffee or tea. Roasted beans, cinnamon and vanilla filled the air. Roach, his target, true to his name, butted in line, getting in front of three other people, making them shake their heads and leave in disgust. Connor dropped in behind Roach, said nothing, and placed his order.

When Roach picked up his drink a few minutes later, things went even further off the rails. "This isn't a macchiato!" he screamed. "I want the manager!" He slammed the cup on the counter, the hot coffee sloshing, drops splashing on Connor's white shirt sleeve.

Connor's face heated. His attention focused on Roach, and everything went into slow motion. He gritted his teeth, a tightness forming under his ear. His hands clenched and unclenched, and he reached for the gun in the holster inside his jacket. He checked his feet, already in position—spread wide, ready to take his shot and blow the guy away. Really? In broad daylight, in a coffee bar inside the Gaylord? *Is this what I'm doing?*

Connor started counting, as the therapist in his anger management class suggested. After three weeks, he'd had to quit the course because he got in a fistfight over a parking space in front of the building and knocked the guy unconscious. He couldn't take the chance of going back—afraid of being arrested. Flashing back on that experience, he realized the counting here at the café had calmed him, and he noticed his breath had evened out. He removed his hand from his still-holstered gun.

Roach hadn't ordered a macchiato like he'd claimed. Still, in situations like this, it's best not to call attention to yourself by defending the barista, even though Connor wanted to. He simply waited for his double espresso and, when his name was called, picked it up, not making eye contact with the barista and stuffing a twenty-dollar bill in her tip jar, relieved he didn't kill his assigned hit in front of witnesses and thankful he'd have no problem pulling the trigger on this prick when it was finally an appropriate time to do so.

Connor walked outside to the atrium and claimed a table by the entrance, with a good view of the coffee shop. He recalled how he bollixed the last job, requiring two extra days to complete it. The problem was, the victim would do nothing to make Connor angry. Finally, on the fourth day, as the target walked his dog, the man dragged it down the sidewalk instead of letting it sniff about and do its business. Connor couldn't abide the mistreatment of animals, and half an hour later he completed his task in a parking garage near the man's place of employment, shooting him twice in the head outside an elevator. On the flight home, he considered retirement but worried his beekeeping hobby would prove too lonely. He needed to be around people, even if he earned a living by killing some of them. "A paradox," he muttered.

Connor stared at Roach's fat, bald, sweaty head framed in the coffeeshop's window and scanned the rest of the scene. He squinted as the sun reflected off big slabs of glass and steel. Besides the OIT (Office of Information Technology) crowd, an abundance of women sat in the atrium and filled it with laughter and light. They wore lanyards too. RWA, they read. He pondered what the letters might stand for. He enjoyed the company of women, not just the sexual interlude but the conversation and the sound of their voices. He studied each one, sipping on his coffee until...

"See anything you like?" a woman asked, smirking down at him. She wore tortoise-shell schoolmarm glasses that took up most of her face, and her hair was knotted into a bun on top of her head. She reminded him of his kindergarten teacher at Bailey Elementary in Dublin many years ago.

"Excuse me?" Connor asked. His heart beat faster, as his eyes blinked quickly and his trigger finger twitched.

"I caught you," she said, shaping one hand into a gun and pointing it at him.

*Fuck me. Is this woman a cop?* Connor searched for an exit. *Should I bring my weapon out? Make a run for it?*

Her smile grew broader and it finally clicked. She's joking. Connor's shoulders relaxed, and he flopped back in his chair. He wished she'd bend down a little lower, so he could get a better view of her cleavage in the purple sweater she wore. He looked past her glasses and examined her cornflower blue eyes, lively with wrinkles at the edges. His mum used to keep cornflowers in a pot on their front stoop. This woman had a pretty face for an older one. *What am I talking about? She's younger than I am.*

"Afraid to tell me?" she said, tilting her head sideways.

"Have we met?" Connor asked.

The woman made a large *haar haar* sound.

"Not likely, unless you're here for the conference. Are you?"

"No, I am not." Her laugh was comical. Connor had to force himself not to laugh at her. A hit man's conference was a novel idea, and Connor could make another fortune if he threw one, but the agency would never allow it.

"Pleasure, then?" she asked.

"Something like that." It would be a pleasure taking Landon Roach down, for sure. It most likely would be a pleasure knowing this woman as well. "What does RWA stand for?" he asked, reading her lanyard. "Wait, I'll guess. Runaway Women Athletes?"

*Haar haar.* Her shoulders jostled as she laughed. "No, Romance Writers of America."

"They have a whole conference for creating titillating stories, do they?"

She tilted her head back. *Haar haar haar!* "I like your accent. Where are you from, Britain or Ireland?"

"Good guess. The second one." He enjoyed hearing her laugh, but she asked too many questions. Did she maybe work for a law enforcement agency? He glanced around at different tables. Was anyone observing them? She'd pushed him off his game. Now he'd divulged he's from Ireland. Get control of the situation. "I'm sorry, I need to go. We can chat later." *Leave the table, eejit.*

"Sure, that would be lovely. I'm Rylee Reed." She stuck out her hand as he stood.

"I know. I read your tag," he replied, taking hold of her hand. "I'm CJ." He noticed she didn't have a ring on her finger. "Grand chatting." He walked away even more angry at himself. *Christ, now you've gone and told her your name too. Now you'll have to marry or kill her.* Connor shook his head and looked skyward. If Pally could see him, he'd be rolling in his grave.

Connor let the escalator carry him to the upper level of the atrium, taking a step occasionally before reaching the top and gliding off. He continued to observe the woman. No one else approached Rylee Reed, so she didn't appear to have a partner. Smooth the way she forced him to give up his name. At least he'd only given his initials, or he might have an even bigger problem on his hands. In all his years of doing this, no one had ever approached him while he stalked a mark.

Not a glamour girl. Not a girl at all. A woman. He would've guessed a different cover—a librarian or a yoga instructor. She removed some books and a notebook from a bag and placed them on the table. She read one of the books and wrote in her notebook as she drank her coffee, so it appeared she might have told the truth about the writing. He imagined Rylee using her books for yoga blocks and snickered. She had one of those long skirts women favored but men like him hated. The slit up the side was alright, allowing one of her legs to reveal itself, but the cut didn't go up high enough. Well-formed calves, though. She was in her late forties, with a curvy body and a nice chest. Connor hoped she wasn't one of these women who was always watching her weight. He liked a little extra meat on the bone. The glasses had to go, though...did she need them, or were they a prop to make her appear more literary? She should let her hair free. He imagined it hanging down while she was on top of him and—

"Check it out," a teenage boy shouted as he whooped and danced, getting down on his knees and popping up again, attempting a dance trick. At the same time, another one filmed him with his camera. Connor gave them the evil eye, but it had no effect. Instead, they got louder. The one filming screamed, "Do it again!"

Connor stood up. "You're too loud. Quiet down."

"Lighten up," the boy filming said. "We're just having fun. It's a public place, not a library."

In no mood for a back-talking little twerp, Connor moved closer, his hand already folded into a fist. A young girl with a shaved head wearing combat boots came up from behind the two boys. "Control yourself. You're worked up over nothing," she said and walked closer, staring Connor down and shaking her finger at him. "If you're upset over something, deal with your own emotions, but don't take it out on us."

"Let's leave," the boy filming said. "We can finish our video somewhere else."

"You're right. Let him live with his own miserable self," the girl said, flipping her hand in the air. The two boys walked away with the girl following them. She turned once and shot Connor a cool-eyed stare.

He remembered Rylee's eyes. They danced when she looked at him. She reminded him of Clover. There was something very feline about Rylee Reed, cautious, but wanting his attention just the same. Rylee's eyes would have displayed displeasure if she'd seen Connor's interaction with this group. He'd lost his cool. They were kids, not targets. He grimaced, took a deep breath, and felt a pain in the back of his throat. He shifted his attention back to the window. *Where the hell did Roach go?*

Connor had lost him. He reminded himself that this wasn't the right way to do things. The old man wouldn't have approved. "Keep your mind on business and your eyes on the target at all times," Pally would have said. Of course, he always had a story to illustrate his point and was a patient teacher. Pally acted nothing like his father had been.

Connor scanned the crowd and spotted Roach near the bar at a larger table with colleagues. Last night, the man had hit the clubs inside the complex hard and seemed to favor vodka. Hopefully, tonight will be the same, making it easy for Connor to complete the job.

His eyes drifted back to Rylee. A man wearing a black trench coat walked up to her, holding a large manila envelope. *Who the hell is he? A boyfriend?* Rylee's mouth sagged downwards as she tossed her head back and forth. She exchanged words with the man and moved her hands about as if swatting off a hoard of bees, refusing to accept what he offered. The man shrugged his shoulders, dropped the envelope on her book, and walked away. She picked it up and opened it slowly, treating the contents like a bomb, wired to explode. She read the papers, shook her head, and after a minute lowered her eyes to the tabletop, bending her head and covering her face with her hands, chest heaving. "No," Connor breathed, rising and sprinting towards the escalator.

# Chapter 2
# Speaking in Maybe's & If's

*"Bees don't come to dead things."*

———Connor Jackson

S he couldn't believe it. Rylee shoved the divorce petition back in the envelope. Her phone vibrated. She glanced down at a text message from the bastard, wiped the tears from her eyes and flipped her glasses down to read.

They said u got them

Don't fight me

It will only lead 2trble

I'm not selling house

Paula likes

Moved ur things 2 storage

I'll give u something if u don't start trble

They'd only separated a month ago, and he'd already filed. *He's taking the house.* She had used all her savings and the inheritance from her grandmother for it. It was a custom build in Greenville, Delaware, two acres sitting in the 19807 zip code. He expected her to just walk away.

*Ring. Ring.* Her caller ID revealed her lifeline and best friend.

"Hey, Sheila," she said.

*Pause.*

"Yes, went to my first session, Keywords on Amazon. Ended at three. I'm taking a break, having some coffee."

*Pause.*

"I'm overwhelmed, is all. You know I don't do well with crowds and need my quiet time."

*Pause.*

"I just feel like a fraud."

*Pause.*

"Because I am. These other authors have series and backlists. I've got one book and it's hasn't even been released."

*Pause.*

"You're my friend, of course you'd say that. There's something else going on with me too."

*Pause.*

"How did you guess? Served me with divorce papers."

*Pause.*

"Just now...the petition said I abandoned him. Is that crazy or what?"

*Pause.*

"By attending this conference, I guess. No, there's nothing about his adultery."

*Pause.*

"He sent a text too. Said he's taking my house and he put my things in storage."

*Pause.*

"Doesn't seem fair to me, either. I love that house and it's devastating to think I won't be able to live there anymore. He expects me to just skulk away because I'm old and worn-out, and he's found a younger version." She choked up and couldn't talk.

*Pause.*

"It's a sweet offer, Sheila, but you live in a studio apartment. And truthfully, you know I need a place of my own. I was planning on traveling, anyway. I'll just start earlier, or I'll rent something."

*Pause.*

"You could be right. No more arbitration. I need my own attorney because he's not going to play fair.

*Pause.*

"I need to be careful. He's capable of anything and right now I'm dependent on him."

*Pause.*

"You're right, Sheila. I need to do something fun, and believe me, I'm trying. A few minutes ago, I went up to a good-looking stranger and chatted him up."

*Pause.*

"You're right, it *doesn't* sound like me. Who am I, Kelly Ripa? Who knows why I did it."

*Pause.*

"Funny but true. I do like my make-believe boyfriends, the ones I write about, better. But I have my reasons. They can shape-shift into anyone I want them to be. I don't have to share them or introduce them to family and friends. And I can control the conversation, because I speak for both of us. And best of all, I don't have to cook them dinner." *Haar haar.* "And when I want them gone, I just stop thinking about them and close my notebook."

*Pause.*

"I guess the difference this time is he's real and attractive—tall, in good shape—and there was something...a confidence about him. He brought something out in me. Just for a moment I became someone else, someone important, worth listening to."

*Pause.*

"I don't know about that. What the hell do I know about sex if I can't even hold my marriage together?"

*Pause.*

"I can't blame David for everything. Maybe if I didn't have an eating—"

*Pause.*

"Or if I did what he wanted, he wouldn't be with a twenty-five-year-old plaything. Maybe if I didn't start writing, if—"

*Pause.*

"You're right, I need to stop speaking in maybes and ifs. I'm working on my issues, and I have a right to follow my passion. I need to stop thinking about David and start thinking about me. Thank God I have you as a friend to talk sense into me."

*Pause.*

"Yes, of course I'm eating. Did I look like I was starving when I left? I still wear a size ten."

*Pause.*

"Thank you for listening to my mental diarrhea and having my back. Love you, Sheila."

Breath. *Come up for air, Rylee.* She fires off a text to David:

> I put u through law school

> I was ur paralegal for ten years
> w/little pay

I used my inheritance to help build the house

I'm hiring an attorney to protect my interests.

* * *

Connor hid behind the enormous pillar near the side of Rylee's table and listened. He overheard her conversation as she spoke on the phone with her friend. Her husband was behind the tears. Another asshole the world could do without. Unfortunately, it didn't work that way. Connor wasn't allowed to kill without orders. The agency frowned on men who went rogue.

Connor chuckled when Rylee Reed discussed her make-believe boyfriends and described him as good-looking. Maybe she did need those glasses after all, but somehow she had seen through his cloak of invisibility. *Secret powers?*

He watched her eyes turn fiery after she said goodbye to her caller and typed a message on her cell. After Rylee put her phone away, Connor approached her. "I told you I'd be back," he said, handing over his white linen handkerchief.

"How much did you hear?" she asked, grasping hold of the handkerchief and glancing back at the pole, as her face turned red in embarrassment.

"Not too much, 'Kelly Ripa.' For being worn and old, you look fabulous," he said, winking.

*Haar, haar.* "Thank you cheering me up," she said, wiping a tear away.

"Would you like some tea, another cup of coffee?" As Connor waited for her answer, he caught movement out of the corner of his eye. Roach had left his table and was walking towards the Belvedere lobby bar, also located in the atrium.

"No thank you. I think I need to work off my anxiety," she said. "I was thinking of going for a swim or maybe hitting the gym."

Connor lowered his eyes back to Rylee. He had ideas for helping Rylee work off her anxiety, but they could never involve water and wouldn't involve treadmills or barbells. He'd much prefer escorting her to his room and—

"I think I'm headed for the pool," she said, returning his handkerchief. "Meet me there if you're interested." Damn, he'd waited too long to answer and now Rylee was leaving and going to the one place he would never go, ever. Connor brought the cloth to his nose and inhaled. Lavender, soft and powdery. It reminded him of Ireland and his mum. He folded the cloth, stuffed it in the inside pocket of his jacket, and watched Rylee until she disappeared. He liked what he'd seen so far. Her husband didn't appreciate what he had if he had showed her the door. Everyone ages, that's a fact.

Connor left the table and headed to the Belvedere. He found a seat at the bar and pulled Rylee's wallet from his pants pocket. It had taken him only seconds to lift it from her bag when she'd buried her eyes into his handkerchief. Rylee really should have a zipper or a snap on that tote. He wistfully remembered his mother, stroking his hair and kissing his head, saying in a sing-song voice, "Yer a dutiful son, taking care of Mum." She was always pleased with whatever Connor had brought home after pick-pocketing tourists after school.

He thumbed through her wallet until he found her Delaware license. Date of birth, February 10, 1970. Old and worn at fifty-two? What did that make him at sixty-four? Ready for the grave? Connor didn't expect her home base to be so close. She lived in Wilmington, only a three-hour drive from the hotel. He examined the rest of Rylee's identification. She's a member of two art museums and Longwood Gardens. She loves culture and gardening; he loves those things too. She travels light and carries only two cards, a Platinum American Express and a bank debit card. There was no type of law enforcement ID present, but there was a small cardboard folder with the logo of the Gaylord and her room number written on the outside. It held one keycard. Since they gave Connor two keycards when he checked in, she most likely had another one in her purse. He'd have kept the bank cards and made a visit to her room, if he weren't a gentleman. Instead, he placed the wallet in his jacket near his heart, called the front desk, and had them transfer the call to her room. "CJ here, room 2022. I found your wallet. Perhaps we can meet, and I can return it."

*Brrrrr.* Connor's phone vibrated with an incoming text. He flipped the phone over and read the message from Archie, his handler as he monitored Lyndon Roach, who sat across from him.

new job

will call soon w/details.

What's wrong with these people? He hadn't completed this one yet. Connor required downtime between assignments and had no interest in doing another bloke so soon.

He had a more immediate problem, though—Roach. He appeared drunk, talking loudly, arguing and attracting attention. This was an upscale bar, not a local dive where they were used to these kinds of things. The sun was just beginning to set over the Potomac River and he could see it through the glass panels in all of its glorious shades of tangerine and red. Things didn't get any better with Roach when twenty minutes later he swung at someone's jaw and landed it. The bouncer hustled him to the front of the bar and summoned the police. The victim pressed charges, and within minutes they had arrested him for drunk and disorderly conduct. As they handcuffed and dragged Roach away, he threatened lawsuits and knocked over two club chairs.

"Shit," Connor said, covering his eyes. He refused to watch anymore. There was no way he could complete the hit on Roach tonight. He signaled the server. He'd have one drink, and with a bit of Irish luck find the Rylee woman and invite her out.

* * *

Rylee wrestled with the elastic fabric, tugging and pulling before finally getting it on. She poked the baggy skin on her thighs with her fingers as she looked in the mirror. Why did she have to look so bad in bathing suits? *You've lost eighty pounds. Stop being a masochist and get yourself in the pool.* But she couldn't leave the locker room, worried about what other people would think of how she looked. *Stop it! People don't care. They have their own issues. Say some affirmations...* "I'm healthy," she began saying out loud to herself. "I can move with ease. My body is strong. I'm healthy. I can move with—"

"Whoops. I'm sorry. I didn't see you," a white-haired woman said while she turned a corner in the locker room using a walker.

"Not your fault, I'm daydreaming," Rylee said, as she clutched her towel and stood by the row of lockers.

"Hopefully, lovely daydreams," the woman said. "You're attending the conference, aren't you?"

"Yes, I am. Just doing affirmations. Telling myself I'm okay."

"You're more than that. We were at the same table, during the Virgin's Journey presentation, don't you remember?" the woman asked.

"Yes, forgive me for not recognizing you."

"In the workshop, we only had ten minutes to brainstorm a plot, and yours was fantastic. I couldn't have done better myself. It impressed everyone at the table. I looked you up as soon as I got back to my room. Saw your debut novel, *Notes from Noel*, is coming out with C&D this fall. Congratulations."

"Well, I guess—"

"You need to stop guessing, darling, and have some confidence in yourself and embrace your success," she said, touching her shoulder. "I'm meeting someone for an interview and I'm late, or I'd stop and chat longer." Then the woman sped away. *Couldn't have done better myself*, the grandmotherly woman had said. Who was this woman? Rylee should have asked her name. She herself had thought the plot she created was too convoluted. *A divorcee attending a conference meets a bad guy, a killer, who actually turns out to be a good guy. Campy trash.*

Rylee entered the pool area, walked down the concrete steps and immersed herself in the cool water. It instantly erased all the tension from the day, and just like always, Rylee lost herself in the buoyant liquid as she swam and counted off each lap. She had started swimming after her therapist suggested it. It helped her deal with anxiety and her eating disorder. Rylee still didn't believe she had one. How could eating healthy be wrong? But according to her therapist, she had something called orthorexia—an obsession with healthful eating.

Rylee hoped CJ would come. He was older than David, but he had a sense of humor and everything about him was real. She liked his accent and gray hair; he didn't color it or turn his skin orange while lying in a tanning booth, like David. She admired his style. He dressed in comfortable but upscale business casual. When she tried to buy clothes like that for David, he laughed and called her stupid. "Attorneys don't wear business casual," he said. CJ worked out, too. She noticed his muscles through his shirt. David refused. He relied on plastic surgery. David was all about shortcuts.

Rylee's stomach growled again. She had eaten lunch and should've eaten more, but everything they served had something wrong with it; the lettuce wasn't organic, the vegetables could've been exposed to pesticides, the dressing was full of preservatives. They brought out cookies at the break, and they looked delicious, but again, full of ingredients she couldn't consume. *Not clean.* Everyone else ate the cookies, but not her. Rylee spent most of her day denying herself food, and the rest of it fixated on what she had eaten or not eaten. *Is this my life?*

She'd been in the water for an hour. *CJ's not coming. Get out before you turn into a prune.* He must've concluded she's a drama queen. Rylee dug down deep for an affirmation. "I'm lovable. I'm interesting." She paused. "I'm out of my mind."

# Chapter 3
# Destiny

Rylee left the water. Walking up the concrete steps, she felt heavier. She picked up the towel from the lounger, wrapped it around her body and headed towards the locker room, shaking her head. *Is that little girl eating chocolate-covered peanuts?* Rylee used to love those. Liar—she loved them still. If she had some, she would eat all of them, search for more and make herself sick. But peanuts and peanut butter are high in aflatoxins. Aflatoxins are toxic byproducts of a fungal metabolism and can cause cirrhosis and hepatitis B, and lead to the development of carcinoma of the liver. *Stop thinking the worse of everything and get dressed. I control my destiny; I control my destiny; I control my destiny.*

* * *

"Drinking is never a good idea while on the job," old Pally used to say. Connor allowed himself just one after calling the police station earlier and learning Roach wouldn't make bond until the morning. After leaving the bar, he walked through the atrium, searching for something to eat. *Ring, ring.* He stopped walking, leaned against the outside wall of a women's clothing boutique, and glanced at the caller ID on his cell. His handler's initial flashed. He pressed answer.

"What's going on with Lyndon Roach?" Archie asked.

"Got arrested. I'll complete when he's released."

"Disappointing, but it happens. Got something else. A new one. At the same place."

"Wait, another one here, at the Gaylord?" Connor asked.

"Affirmative."

"Not sure—"

"I thought this'd be a no-brainer for you," Archie interrupted. "Cuts down on travel time and expenses. Do the first one, immediately do the next and get the hell out of Dodge. Waiting on Hubie to send her pic. I'll provide all the details in the morning."

"A woman?" Connor asked, inhaling and holding his breath.

"Yeah, husband wants it to look like a slip in the tub, an overdose, a fall over a railing, something like that," his handler said. "Be creative. Accident clause in the life insurance policy. Bonus if done that way. I'll text in the morning." The line went dead.

Connor stuffed his phone into his pocket. He'd never done a woman before, whether by fate, accident, or the agency deliberately not assigning them to him because of his history. He wiped the film of sweat from his forehead. His breathing came faster. Light-headed, he leaned against the outside of the building, waiting for his dizziness to subside. Memories flooded back from that day, forty-four years ago, when he found her on the floor. *I didn't protect her.*

Connor straightened up and willed himself to walk through the giant atrium, pushing the image of his mother's bloody body from his mind. As he moved, he considered eating at the different restaurants he passed. Maybe that was the problem. If he ate something, his dizziness would disappear. He came to an abrupt stop when his eyes landed on Rylee Reed. She called to Connor like the only life raft in an ocean miles from shore.

"How was the swim?" Connor asked, walking closer.

"Ahh, lovely," she said, as her cheeks and ears turned red. She wrapped her arms around herself protectively.

"Sorry I didn't join you. I had a task to complete," Connor said. "Did you get my message earlier, by the way?"

"No, I'm sorry, I didn't. What was it?" Rylee's eyebrows drew together, and she leaned closer to Connor in anticipation.

"I found your wallet underneath the table." He pulled it from his coat pocket and passed it to her. "I left my number for you to call."

"Oh my gosh. I didn't know this was missing," she said, placing the wallet back inside the bag and then covering her mouth with a hand and shaking her head. "What a hassle if I would have to replace this. I can't thank you enough."

"Yes you can. Join me for dinner, so I don't have to dine alone." Connor smiled. He thought about how soft her hands were and the fact that she was too trusting. Rylee didn't even check the contents.

"I guess I should," she smirked, "to express my appreciation."

Connor liked it when she smiled like that. "What's your favorite food?" he asked.

"Sushi, but I'm particular because—"

"I know a great place, don't worry," Connor said as he took her elbow and steered Rylee towards the lobby.

* * *

"It was smart of you to call from the Uber and get a reservation," Rylee whispered to him as they waited in line to be seated.

"Oishi's has a stellar reputation," Connor said. "I'm surprised they could—"

"What do you mean, you have nothing available?" a man in front of them yelled while gesturing at the hostess.

"I'm sorry, sir, but—" the hostess started to explain before being interrupted.

"I spend thousands of dollars here every month when I bring guests for business, and now you can't find my girlfriend and me a table?" His face turned red, and his diamond earring reflected and bounced an orange color from the overhead spotlight.

"If you'd like to put your name on the list, and something opens up, I'll—"

"I don't want to put my name on any list," he screamed, waving his fist in the air.

Connor walked up to the desk and pulled the man aside. "Don't put your name on the list. Leave," he ordered, his face flushed and hands clenching.

The man jerked his head away, his mouth opened and eyes widened. "I won't be back here, ever. Count on it." He turned his back on the hostess and stormed out the door with his girlfriend running to keep up.

Connor returned to his place in line. "People complain about how rude the French are, but Americans' behavior and self-entitlement is worse, don't you think?"

"It could be we eat too many cheeseburgers," Rylee said. *Haar haar*. "Maybe he was having a bad day. You can't judge a person by one incident."

"I think you can tell a lot about a person by how they treat those in the service industry. Bad behavior has become a common practice. People think they can act out and get away with it."

Rylee looked away. "You're right, but I don't like confrontation."

"Sometimes you have to call people on their actions."

"I understand, but I try to look at things from a different perspective. Like I said, maybe they're having a bad day." Then

Rylee changed the subject. "I love the way this place is decorated. Lots of light quartz, walnut wood, and the low lighting. It's sophisticated."

"Definitely," Connor said.

Rylee knew her way around the sushi menu but she seemed to have an inordinate amount of dietary concerns, excluding potential items on the menu one after another for various reasons. It got even stranger when the server came to take their order. Rylee asked him where the fish came from, whether it was mercury-free, and if they rinsed the rice before cooking it. Connor thought he saw the server's eyes roll. As her questions continued to mount, Connor touched her arm gently. "I'll order for both of us, if that's alright," and watched as she shifted in her seat and then breathed a sigh of relief.

She stammered, "I'm sorry...I watch what I eat. I'm cautious and sometimes it gets the better of me."

Connor ordered the special, twenty pieces of nigiri for both of them to share, and said, "If you don't like what I ordered after it arrives, you can order something else, okay?"

When the server presented the platter, Rylee gushed about the artistry. "This is too beautiful to eat," she said.

"I don't have a problem," Connor said, picking up a piece with his chopsticks and dipping it into a soy sauce and wasabi mixture before shoving it into his mouth. "Delicious."

"Connor, I didn't take a picture of the plate for Instagram yet," she laughed. "Now the symmetry is off."

"Don't worry," Connor said, taking another piece from the opposite side and making her smile.

They spent three hours discussing and sampling sushi, drinking tea and talking. Connor noticed he'd eaten most of it, no matter how much he encouraged her to eat more. "You didn't eat much and skipped all the ones with rice," Connor said.

"Yes, I did, ah...rice can have arsenic."

"Are you kidding?"

"No. If it's not rinsed properly, it can increase your risk of cancer, diabetes and heart disease," Rylee said. He flashed her a look of disbelief, chuckled, and scratched his jaw. Most men in his line of work were dead by his age. They either ate their gun or someone else put them down. How much rice would he have to eat to die from arsenic poisoning?

Rylee changed the subject. "I love to travel. I'm going to do a lot this year. When I graduated from college, I took six months and traveled all over Europe, hosteling and writing about it. It was the best time of my life. I haven't traveled since then. That's why I'm going to Cuba in the fall and after I return, I'll take a couple months and visit Asia, too. I can write while I travel." Connor liked to travel too. His occupation allowed him to do a lot of it. He never knew where they would send him, and he enjoyed that unpredictability.

"Why have you waited so long?" he asked.

Rylee took in a deep breath and glanced down at the table. Her smile wavered. She opened and then closed her mouth as if choosing the right words, "Ah, my soon-to-be ex never wanted to take time from his practice, and I worked there too. It just—umm, never happened." Her voice grew quieter. "It wasn't all his fault. I could have if I wanted to. What do you do, CJ?"

He had expected this question all evening. He guessed Rylee had been saving it for dessert. "Problem solver, mostly," he said, looking her in the eye, leaning over the table to get closer.

"Computers or what, exactly?"

"No, more personal than that. Unfortunately, I can't really discuss the details." That response usually stopped further questions from his date.

Rylee nodded slightly. "I see." Her eyes narrowed, and her brow wrinkled. She scooted her chair back from the table, further away from him. Connor could see he'd raised her suspicions of him. He needed to bring her back.

"I spend a lot of time on my hobby," he said.

"What's that?"

"I keep bees."

"Really?" Rylee's eyes grew enormous, and a small smile spread on her lips. "How interesting." She slid forward in her chair. "I have some questions." Her eyes stared intensely at him.

"Would you like to come back to my room for a drink?" Connor asked. "I'll tell you everything about them."

\* \* \*

They walked down the corridor together, past the hallway lined with mirrors. Who was the woman reflected there? Rylee wanted to laugh or scream. She couldn't believe she'd agreed to come to CJ's room. For once, she refused to be the play-it-safe, by-the-rules kind of person she'd always been. She'd become Noel, the heroine in her romance novel—a risk taker. *Is this who I am?*

CJ held her hand, his large, feverish fingers wrapped around hers tightly. They entered the elevator. He made the car seem small because he's so big. He scanned his key card and selected the twentieth floor. As soon as the doors closed, he climbed all over her, gathering her in his arms, pushing her against the wall and bringing his hands to her hips. She wondered if there were cameras in the elevator and glanced up, searching, but only found his eyes. "Are you frightened?" he asked.

"Should I be?" Rylee realized no one but David had kissed her in twenty-seven years, and he'd never kissed her in an elevator even once.

CJ flipped a switch labeled "emergency stop" on the panel and the elevator came to an abrupt halt. "I'd never hurt you, and I won't do anything without your permission." He stared into her eyes and then down at her mouth. Rylee didn't want him to ask for permission. She wanted CJ to take charge and push forward, and he must have heard her even though she didn't speak the words. His tongue slid into her mouth, so soft as it wrapped around hers and the two danced lazily. She hoped the sushi didn't make her breath taste bad, but the thought was quickly pushed away when his kiss turned savage. His lips slammed down harder, and his tongue became a weapon as he sliced and invaded her mouth like an alien attempting to probe and devour her. He moved one of his hands to the back of her head and brought her forcefully towards him, his hard body pressed into hers. He pulled away and stared at her. "Are we okay?"

*Did he notice my hesitancy? Does he know I don't know what I'm doing?* Rylee's face heated, and her heart raced. CJ's accent was so damn sexy, and he smelled good too, like the woods and lemons. "I'm good," she said. Connor flipped the stop button the other way and they resumed their journey. Still holding her head, Connor took his other hand, grabbed her rear, and pulled her closer, pressing into her, making Rylee feel his erection against her inner thigh. David had never displayed this kind of passion toward her.

"You feel good. I could take you right here," he said, making Rylee's pulse quicken.

*What will he think when I take my clothes off?* Her body was nothing like the women in the *Sports Illustrated* Swimsuit Edition. *Stop it.* She could always ask CJ to dim the lights. Few people have perfect bodies, after all.

The elevator door opened. She grinned. *He'll think I'm deranged. I am.* They walked down the corridor together, past the hallway lined with mirrors. She didn't recognize herself anymore when she looked into them. She missed her old body and wasn't sure about the new one, even though everyone seemed to prefer her new shape better. David hadn't liked the old her, had called her fat, but he didn't like the new one any better, it seemed.

They stood outside of his room, number 2022. CJ waved the card and opened the door. "Welcome, Rylee," he said, holding her hand. She clutched her purse to her chest and hovered by the door, like a rabbit deciding whether to run or hope the fox only inches away had forgotten her.

# Chapter 4
# Easy Honey

"There's no such thing as easy, honey."

— —Unknown

"Are you comin' in, then, lovely?" CJ asked. Frozen, he stared at her as if the slightest movement would scare her away, but she couldn't run. It was as if her feet couldn't touch the floor. Rylee floated into the room instead. "Stay in the present," she mouthed as the door closed quietly behind her.

The room was immense, a whole suite. CJ's smile was huge. "Would you like something to drink?" he asked, his teeth white and perfect. When she didn't answer, he removed his black jacket and unbuttoned his white Oxford shirt. His teeth matched his shirt. *What a stupid thing to notice.* CJ didn't shave his chest like David. She liked that he didn't. She wanted to touch his chest and his wiry silver chest hair. *I'm crazy. Is this a mistake?*

He caught her staring. "Are you going to write about this?" he asked as his eyes gleamed and danced. She hadn't noticed how gray his eyes were before.

"If it's any good," she replied. *Who am I? Have I turned into Noel, the heroine of my story?*

"Then I better pony up," CJ said and smiled. He captured her hands, held her body against the wall, placed one hand on her neck, and stared deeply into her eyes. "Could we lose the glasses for a bit?" he asked. "I want to see yer eyes." She nodded her head because her voice had disappeared. He brought both hands to either side of her head, then her ears, and gently stripped the glasses from her face. Chills traveled up and down her neck. He rested her glasses gently on the table, returned, and retook her hands.

Not being able to see had pushed her further inside herself. She second-guessed her decision, and her mind raced, landing on different thoughts: she should have worn a lacier pair of panties, wait until she's officially divorced, she didn't really know CJ well enough to be in his room, and what would her priest say about her actions? *I'm not good enough or sexy enough for him.* Her mind churned, a hurricane of crazy thoughts that crashed into one another. He dropped her hands, touched her shoulders, and stared. "You've gone quiet, and your eyes.... Is something wrong?"

"I'm sorry. I can't do this now...I made a mistake coming up here." She backed up and twisted her fingers. CJ's face crumpled for a second before he gained control. She expected anger. That's how David reacted when she didn't do what he wanted. CJ tilted his head to one side, and their eyes met, but he appeared all fuzzy.

"Something you ate? Something I did?" he asked, sounding concerned.

"No. Nothing like that." She couldn't meet his gaze, and perspiration formed under her arms. She cleared her throat. "I'm not ready. It's too soon. I thought I could." She stammered, "I...I'm sorry I misled you."

"Don't apologize. If that's how you feel, that's how it is." CJ crossed over to the table and retrieved her glasses. The rhythm of his footsteps aligned with the beat of her heart. She wanted to change her mind after CJ handed them to her, but she knew she'd already ruined the evening. She put her glasses on, and when she lifted her head and saw him, his image was clear and in focus again, his mouth turned downward. "I'll walk you to your room," he said, putting his white shirt back on and buttoning it. There was no time to slide her hands in and touch his chest hair. CJ patted her arm reassuringly. She couldn't swallow and choked back tears. *What am I afraid of? Making a mistake again? Not being good enough?*

"I'm sorry," she said, taking his arm. "There must be something wrong with me." She lowered her head so as not to look at him.

"I don't think so," CJ said gently. He brought one hand under her chin, guiding her head up, looked into her eyes and smiled. "You're smart, sweet and sexy." Then he kissed her lips and nuzzled her neck. The hairs on his jaw scratched and made her shiver. He nipped her neck and made her flinch, but Rylee clung to his shoulders, afraid to let go. "I thought you wanted to leave?" he whispered in her ear.

"I don't know..." She backed up and stared into his eyes as her own wavered back and forth, her whole body trembling.

"I do," Connor said and dived back in, kissing her deeply and grasping her wrist tightly so she couldn't move away. He pushed her against the wall again, placed his leg between hers, and thrust his other hand underneath her skirt, between her legs, reaching her underwear. She doesn't stop him this time. Once there, he chuckled, "Damn, yer wet, woman. These panties are damp. Yer body wants me, even if yer mind is telling you something different. Maybe just once, shut yer mind off and give yer body what it wants," he suggested, his fingers and her panty's fabric rubbing against her. Rylee didn't want to like it, but she did and moved against his hand and groaned. "I'd get down there right now and eat that wet pussy, but since yer a shy one, I'd best do it this way," Connor said in a throaty voice. Rylee felt her face burn, but she rocked against his hand. He pinched her clit through the fabric of her panties, and when she pulled away, it stretched her underwear enough for Connor to slide his hand underneath them. Now his hot, calloused fingers were on her pussy. Distracted by his words but still on fire and reeling from the pinch, Connor forced a finger wet with her juices into her pussy and circled her clit with his thumb. It had been so long since she'd had sex with anyone, even herself, that he had her rocking on his hand within minutes. Connor continued to push his finger in deeper as her body demanded more. Eventually, his finger was in all the way and she, so needy for release, found herself slamming down on him. He answered her need and shoved a second finger in. "You feel delicious," he said, pushing that one more fiercely, filling her up as he continued circling her clit harder until an orgasm roared through her.

"C-JAAAAAAAAY!" she screamed as she convulsed against his hand and leg, pinned against the wall by Connor's frame, his free hand still wrapped around her wrist, not letting go.

"Good girl," Connor said, encouraging her, as he continued to fuck her with his fingers until her pussy stopped clenching and unclenching around them, her head burrowing into his chest and his chest hair tickling her, tears flowing down her face. *I am good enough...*

* * *

Friday

Connor opened his eyes. The blue morning sky filled the room, and the color matched Rylee's eyes exactly. He groaned and threw a pillow over his face. Somehow, she'd crawled into his brain. He'd wanted more from her last night, but she turned out different than he'd anticipated. When she first approached him at his table in the atrium, she had seemed forward and assertive. Connor hadn't expected the vulnerability she'd revealed to him in his room. When she'd cried after he got her off, he was afraid he'd hurt her, but she'd insisted no and whispered, "I didn't know it could be like that." He would like to see her again, but it might be a mistake— she wasn't a woman you bang once and walk away from, but he didn't live a life that allowed for long-term commitments. Pally advised staying unattached and using call girls. "It's not a good idea to get close to anyone," he once preached, taking a drag off one of those cigars he favored. "At some point, they could learn what you do. Loose lips sink ships." Pally lived what he preached and would have died alone if Connor hadn't arrived at the hospital in time.

He didn't close the drapes the night before, wanting to lose himself in the night sky and remember how Rylee Reed called his name, and the surprise in her eyes when she came. He'd been able to make her come fast and had enjoyed every moment of it. He loved the smell and feel of her. She was good company, too, even if she had some crazy dietary concerns and notions. Connor wanted to give her another orgasm, but unfortunately she had left his room embarrassed. Now the sun had woken him; or was it his erection? His phone vibrated, announcing a text message. He picked it up off the nightstand and read the text from Archie about his new assignment.

Rylee Reed

rm 1826

see link w/pic.

Did Connor read it correctly? "It can't be," he muttered, his erection gone. He bolted up and opened the link, staring at the photograph. Rylee Reed stared back at him, the same woman he'd taken to dinner and given an orgasm to last night. "Fuck no!" he screamed, heaving the phone across the room and hitting the wall. It ricocheted halfway back to him and landed on the beige carpet. He jumped from the bed and retrieved it; a miracle the cell was still intact and hadn't broken into pieces. His arms went limp, and a stabbing chest pain forced him to take deeper breaths. Was he having a heart attack? He sat there a moment and waited for his body to settle down, then paced around the room and slammed his fists against the wall several times, making the pictures on the wall jump. Someone thumped back. Connor contemplated marching next door and killing them. He had an itch he couldn't scratch, but he held himself back, counted to twenty, and gained control over his anger. "This can't be happening, it can't," he muttered. *I meet a woman I like, and she's my newest mark? Is this another punishment from God?*

Connor had never turned down a job before, mainly because every one of them deserved to be whacked. But not this one. Definitely not this one. What choice did he have? Do the job and cross a line he hadn't crossed before—killing someone who didn't deserve it? Or refuse the job and let someone else do it? What if they bungled it and made her suffer? Should he warn her? *Don't go bonkers.* They'd put a contract out on him if they learned of it, and what would it solve anyway? If they wanted her dead, she was dead. He held his phone and clicked on the link again, reexamining the photograph of Rylee as nausea hit him and a loud scream escaped. He moaned, "Not again," raked his hand through his hair, headed towards the bathroom, and willed himself not to think about the situation.

\* \* \*

Connor wanted his morning fix, his cuppa. He decided no, he needed Irish coffee instead this morning. He stared down from the atrium at all the people below. Rylee Reed was attending a session somewhere, not knowing her time on this earth would soon end. He shoved himself away from the railing and pulled his phone out, scrolling to recent calls and found the one from yesterday. His finger pressed RETURN CALL. He didn't wait for Archie's voice. "CJ here."

"Good news, I hope."

"Not yet. I'm calling about the other one. Don't want it. Increases my liability, plus a woman."

"You shittin' me? I thought you were a pro. Two in one night is nothing for you. And what about Title Nine? Killing's for everyone these days. Are you knocking knees with the broad or something?"

"I'm not accepting the gig. All you need to know," Connor said, disconnecting the call. *I wish I could "knock knees" with Rylee.* How did Archie guess? But he could never see her again. Saving damsels in distress was not in his job description. He returned to his room and packed. He wanted to ensure he was ready to go as soon as he completed the Roach assignment. He wanted to be back in Ireland by the time someone carried out the job on Rylee. He shuddered and pushed the idea away. If he had gone to bed with her, he might be in even worse shape. At least he gave her something nice, an orgasm, before she had to leave this earth. What if the guy they brought in tried to touch her? His face heated, and he balled his fists. "Stop thinking about her," he muttered.

Connor returned to the café, purchased his coffee, walked the atrium, spotted his original target, and followed him into the Belvedere Bar. He settled into the booth, ordered some Irish whiskey from the server, and poured it into his coffee. Pally wouldn't have approved—"Drinking on the job, and in the morning too, not a good move," he could hear him lecturing now.

As he sipped on it, he overheard Roach bragging about how much his bail had cost and how many fights he had won while in jail. *What an asshole.*

"Hi, stranger," Rylee called, waving to him from the doorway. Connor stood up as she moved towards him, bending in and kissing his cheek. She smelled fresh, like his cottage after it rained. *How can I face her? Shit. Control yourself. Smile, dummy.* "I'm in between sessions. I wanted to apologize for letting you down last night." Her face blushed. "I mean...ah, leaving so quickly afterward and—not reciprocating—."

"Who we got here?" Roach asked, interrupting them and wrapping his arm around Rylee's shoulder.

"Ahh, are you speaking to me?" Rylee asked, frowning.

"Yeah. I asked your name."

"Rylee," she said, biting her lip and looking toward Connor as if unsure what to do.

Roach yelled over to the server, "Bring little Rylee a drink on me."

Rylee laughed. "I haven't been little since I was twelve. Thank you, but no, it's too early for me." She moved Roach's arm off her.

"Listen, I'm being a nice guy," he said in a low voice. "Why can't you play nice too and let me buy you a drink? If you don't, I won't be so nice." His eyes narrowed as he stared at her.

Rylee's nose wrinkled, and she squinted through her glasses. "What's wrong with you?"

"He's an asshole," Connor said. Roach swung at him but was either too drunk or so bad at fighting that he ended up grazing Rylee's shoulder instead. It happened so fast that Connor didn't have time to control his rage. The man had touched Rylee. He reacted and punched Roach, bringing him to the floor.

Roach wheezed and grabbed his stomach on folded knees, staring at him in disbelief. "Don't you...know who I am?" Roach asked, huffing as he stared up at Connor.

"Of course, I know who you are. An asshole," Connor said, towering over Roach, getting ready to nail him again. Rylee grabbed the sleeve of his shirt and pulled him away bringing him to his senses. Connor threw some money on the table and took Rylee's hand. "We've got to leave."

"I'm sorry I put you in that position," Rylee said, looking downcast. "I should have realized he was drunk and let him buy me a drink. What's the harm?" she said as they exited the bar.

"Because you don't have to do something you don't want to do to make it easier for someone else," he said. "It never works. Nice guys finish last. Or in your case, nice gals." Rylee needed to learn this or.... Connor stopped himself and grimaced. She didn't need to learn anything. Rylee wasn't long for this world. He let go of her hand.

# Chapter 5
# Kicking the Beehive

"If you want honey, be sweet to your bees."

— —Connor Jackson

Cj walked her to the next workshop, reassuring her about the incident. He used an analogy and called himself the exclamation point. "I made sure you got heard," he said, "and I guarantee, he'll never touch you again."

"I appreciate you standing up for me, but I'm not sure if punching him will serve him long-term."

"It's about protecting you. He touched you. I touched him. Justice was served. An eye for an eye and a tooth for a tooth." CJ's eyes became angry.

"You're quoting the Bible now? How about turning the other cheek?" Rylee asked. "You're not God, and you're also not working for him. Maybe we could have diffused his behavior another way." Her eyes searched his for agreement, but CJ turned away from her and plunked down at a table. People, most of them women, filed in around them. She sat next to him and tried to make eye contact, but he looked down with slumped shoulders. When he did glance up, he stared vacantly into space. "Don't get me wrong. I loved that you stood up for me," she said, touching his hand. "No one ever has." He looked into her eyes, nodded, and squeezed her hand. Neither of them had noticed the doors closing until they became locked. The sound transported Rylee back to the shelter. They always locked them in at night. They had to go there after her father, a successful chiropractor, left her mother and her. Her father had constantly criticized Rylee, her eating, and how she looked and carried herself. She was never good enough. *Is that why he left?*

"Welcome to our workshop on Murder, Forensics 101," someone announced through the microphone, pulling Rylee's attention back to the room. "There is no such thing as perfect evidence," the speaker said, standing in front of an enormous screen. All the conversation in the room tapered off.

"She's got that part right," CJ nodded, unbuttoning his collar. "How am I going to get out of here?" he asked, eying the double doors.

Rylee checked the brochure. "It's only an hour. This author writes suspense and thriller romance." CJ grunted and closed his eyes as if the whole thing was a bore. Rylee wanted to learn from this speaker. If she could be a successful writer, she could take care of herself. "The brochure said she's made over a million dollars with her backlist this year." Her eyes shifted back to CJ and down at his hands. One of his knuckles was scraped and bleeding. She'd caused that. Her eyes drifted up to his lips. They looked so soft. Then their eyes met. *I'm acting like a teenage girl. Stop swooning. Concentrate on what it takes to be successful or end up a failure, dependent on others, like Mom.*

She pulled her eyes to the front of the room and the speaker.

The room was freezing, and she wrapped her arms around herself. Rylee wished they were CJ's. The speaker continued, "Real crime scenes are not like television. Most evidence that normally could've been used in a trial instead gets contaminated at the scene, not on purpose, either by the authorities, the weather or passersby's. Locating a usable piece of evidence is a challenge."

CJ ran a hand through his hair, scratched his arm, and eyed the exit. "Any ideas on how I can leave? I have an appointment."

"What's your last name?" she asked.

"What?"

"Your last name?" she asked softly.

"Jackson."

Rylee raised her hand, and the presenter looked over and pointed, "You have a question?"

"Yes, I'm Rylee Reed, and my friend, ahh...Detective Jackson, wanted to say a few words before leaving to investigate a breaking case." All eyes turned to CJ as he glared back at her.

He stood, buttoned his jacket, and touched his temple. "I wanted to add my thoughts on ballistics," he said. "The barrel has its own unique surface, and almost acts like a fingerprint when fired. There's no strong statistical formula behind finding a match for the gun and bullet, and there's a reason. The bullet must survive whatever it hits, and a person's skull among other things is very hard and can damage a bullet. The other challenge is that professional criminals rarely keep the weapon they commit the crime with, again making evidence collection difficult."

"Thank you, Detective Jackson. Excellent points for all those writing romance thriller and suspense." Everyone clapped, and a few people smiled at him.

"Sure," CJ said and shot Rylee a smirk as he walked towards the door. The door monitor unlocked it and escorted him out. She still didn't know what he did for a living, but it was obvious he knew all about ballistics. Most likely some type of counterintelligence or something like that. Maybe that's why he was bored by the presentation—he knew all about it. Whatever it was, she felt safe with him. Maybe too much so, as she flashed on how she had ridden his leg and hand and orgasmed. Her face heated, and other parts too. David made her tense; she was always on edge, confident he'd done something lousy that she'd soon discover. This put a damper on everything.

Rylee had discovered David was a worm six months after she married him. She'd been stupid. *No, I learn from my mistakes.* They had been returning home one evening after spending the night out with another couple. He was driving his new Jag, drank too much, and hit a pedestrian. He pushed Rylee into the driver's seat before the police arrived or anyone saw him, warning her that their futures were on the line. Luckily, she didn't have to lie because everyone assumed she drove. She also figured out who she was that night—she was someone without a spine. She continued taking orders from David for the next twenty-five years, until last year when she finally stood up to him and "No, David" became her mantra. David was fake, a mirage, and she didn't want to be with someone who wasn't truthful about who they were ever again.

Connor sat in the atrium, keeping his eye on the bar where Roach, his mark, still drank, but he couldn't stop thinking about Rylee and what would soon happen to her. He'd never felt bad about a mark or even given an extra thought about them in the forty-plus years now of doing his job. What's wrong with him? Why now? He tapped his fingers on the table and rubbed the back of his neck. His hands were sweating. He removed his handkerchief from his pocket and wiped them off. *Maybe it's time to hang it up.* He thought about Domenic. He used to be in the business, too, but bailed six years ago, telling no one, not even him. The agency asked Connor several times if he'd heard from Domenic, and Connor always told them no. The truth was, Domenic had called him a month after leaving. He now lived in Seoul, South Korea, with his wife Bora and a new baby girl. He owned a bar and had locals manage it. They talked once a month, shooting the shit about what might have been and the future. Domenic might be around and awake. Connor found the Chat app and started one.

Got a problem, mate

U awake

Connor stared at his phone. No response. He watched as Roach ordered another vodka. Then Connor's phone vibrated, causing his eyes to drop to the cell cradled in his hands.

What's up?

Connor's phone blinked, waiting for his response and he wrote:

Met a woman

Great

No, a problem

Why?

Assigned as mark

Shit

Yeah

Retire. Maybe time, karma

take kitty&go

I live alone

Might B time 2chng tht

always a home4U in SK.

Was Domenic right? Could he just walk away and help Rylee?

THKU later.

Connor pushed the phone back into his pocket. *Do the job,* he told himself. *Kill Roach.* "Stop thinking with your dick," Pally would say. "You're too old for that." He headed towards the escalator and the Belvedere lobby bar.

* * *

*Ring, ring.*

"Hi, Sheila. Yes, things are wonderful. Waiting for the next session to start. Believe it or not, I had a date last night. Yes, with a guy." Laughing. "CJ. No, you can't run a background check on him, I just met him."

*Pause.*

"Not exactly. Does something with security, I think. Yes, he's good-looking and considerate, but it doesn't matter. I can't get involved."

*Pause.*

"You know why. I don't need to worry about it, anyway. I probably won't see him again. I'll explain later."

*Pause.*

"I'm not ready to get back in the saddle. Because I'm not out of the other saddle yet. Yes, we'll talk later. Bye."

Sheila stood by her, no matter what. When David finally confessed to having a mistress, Sheila did everything she could to build Rylee up. When Rylee revealed her longing to write, Sheila encouraged her. If she hadn't, Rylee wouldn't have attempted it. Most of her friends tried to dissuade her. One said, "Look at all the competition, and what do you know about writing?"

*Ring, ring.*

"Hello?"

*Pause.*

"Eric. Is everything alright?"

*Pause.*

"Really? But I thought they were happy with the title. But why now? They've already designed the cover."

*Pause.*

"Yes, I'm having a blast. Can you at least explain why?"

*Pause.*

"I see. I didn't realize the company ran focus groups on books."

*Pause.*

"Of course, I'm happy the publisher sees potential in the book. I understand they want me to think series when selecting the title, but—"

*Pause.*

"Yes, I'll look at the list of choices. Alright, you, too. Thank you, Eric." Most likely he was telling her about this because her editor was too chicken to call. She opened her email and looked at the proposed new titles. Crap, they all made the book sound like a sex manual, not a romance novel.

Rylee's phone vibrated. No respite today. A text from David. What did he want now? She read his message then immediately became angry. *How could he?* She covered her mouth with one hand, reading the text message on her phone, her hand trembling.

> Sorry. Accountant & lawyer agree
>
> Advised me 2 cancel your credit cards
>
> I left U the debit card. Left$200 in the account
>
> Plan & budget, cuz no more coming.

She slammed her phone on the table. How would she pay the hotel bill or anything else? She held her stomach, now suddenly cramping. A heaviness fell over her. Could she even make it to her next session? She remembered what Connor had said about not going along and speaking up. She pressed David's number on her cell and he answered immediately.

"Yes, it's me. Yes, I got the message, but—"

*Pause.*

"You know that's not enough money until I—"

*Pause.*

"Please, David, be reasonable. I have two more days here. I have the hotel to—"

*Pause.*

"The hotel is eight hundred dollars a night, and I have to eat."

*Pause.*

"Yes, I still eat. Can you try not to be mean?"

*Pause.*

"I can't use my advance. I don't have it yet."

*Pause.*

"Don't hang up, please..."

*Pause.*

"David. David? Are you there?"

\* \* \*

This guy's legal bills must be stratospheric. Connor watched as Roach got rowdy again in a crowded bar. It wasn't even one in the afternoon yet, and the guy was blasted. He started something with the patron sitting next to him. Connor rushed toward Roach to keep him from throwing a punch. "Okay, big guy, take it easy," he said as he held Roach's shoulder and maneuvered him towards the exit. Roach was so out of it, he didn't even recognize Connor as the person who punched him earlier in the day. The downside was that a bar full of people witnessed him taking Roach out of there.

He got him into the elevator, found his keycard, and selected his floor, the twenty-second. Connor hadn't planned to do the job then, but he might never get a better opportunity, especially if the guy kept getting arrested.

"I didn't know there would be two of you. I'll have to charge more," the blonde in a red corset and black fishnet stockings said when Connor entered Roach's room, number 2244, throwing him on the bed.

"What did he agree to?" Connor asked, giving her a sideways glance.

"A thousand if I did whatever he wanted for two hours, which he paid for upfront on his credit card, plus a tip." She smiled. "He's already used up an hour."

"Your name, sweetheart?"

"Summer."

Summer could easily turn to fall, but why make things messy? She'd done no harm and wasn't his target. "Here you go, Summer," he said, taking out two hundred and handing it to her. "Keep the money he already paid you and take this extra for your time." Hopefully that would ensure her silence.

After she left, Connor closed the drapes, turned on the television, and pushed the volume up. Back to basics and keep it simple, a tribute to his mentor. Pally believed in surveying the scene and working organically with what was available. Connor grabbed a pillow and approached Roach, now passed out on the mattress, mouth open with snores and gurgling noises emitting. He placed the pillow over his face and put all his body weight on top of him. Roach fought back with his hands, striking out and clawing at Connor, but couldn't reach him or gain leverage. He sunk deeper into the mattress.

The booze had weakened him. He kicked too, but again was unable to make contact. Connor pictured Roach hitting Rylee earlier, which gave him enough angry motivation to push down harder and complete the job, even when the man was fighting for his life. In less than twenty seconds, Roach stopped fighting and let himself go. Connor smelled a foul odor. Most likely, the man had shit himself. He kept the pillow and his weight on him another minute for insurance. After he stood up and removed it, he saw that Roach's eyes and mouth were smiling blankly. Death agreed with Landon Roach the Third. Connor touched his wrist and searched for a pulse. He felt nothing. The body was already cooling.

He went into the bathroom, washed his hands, grabbed a washcloth, and wiped down anything he touched, including the doorknob, keycards and television. He then sent management a text.

Bug eliminated.

# Chapter 6
# Fun & Games

"Bees produce honey and I kill people. We
all have a job to do."

— —Connor Jackson

It wasn't a perfect job—a bar full of people saw Connor leave with the mark—but he had to play the cards he'd been dealt. No one saw him leave Roach's room, no cameras were in that part of the hall, and he used the steps to get to his floor. He walked inside the room, picked up his bag and, using his own key card, took the elevator down to the floor above the atrium.

He glanced over the railing to look at Rylee one more time. He should check out, but watched instead as she drank a coffee, wrote in her notebook, and concentrated. Her eyes focused on her paper and her pen flew across the page. Connor liked how she got a dreamy expression on her face, sequestered in her own little world. Most likely she was writing one of her stories. *Is she writing about what I did to her last night?* He caught himself smiling as he remembered, but when his eyes shifted to the table next to hers, his smile vanished. A dark-haired man in his early thirties was studying her. He didn't belong there. The man wore a European-style suit, cut close to the body with narrow lapels. He stood up and stretched. The suit appeared expensive, charcoal gray, and the pants were hemmed shorter than the typical American style. The man tried hard but wasn't very good at blending in. He pretended to glance at his phone, but his eyes landed on Rylee every few seconds. This had to be the new player the agency hired. *Was it too late for Rylee to escape? Could I take the other guy out from up here? What the fuck? I'm thinking of shooting up the Gaylord again. Have I gone senile?*

"What are you doing here?" Rylee asked, peering up from the table. "I thought you had at a meeting."

Connor flashed a reassuring smile and glanced at the man at the other table. "I got done early," he said, returning his gaze to Rylee.

"Great," Rylee said. "Umm, I have a situation and I don't know how to ask you—"

"Whatever it is, ask me while we walk." Connor glanced over at the table. The man was watching them.

"I'm plotting right now."

"Do it later, luv." He picked up her books, stuffed them into her bag, and handed it to her. He took her hand and led her from the table. "Come, I need to speak to you about something as well." The man got up from his table too.

"Please, I need to ask you *now*. It's important," Rylee said, stopping and staring at him.

*Christ.* "What?" Connor asked, attempting to keep his voice calm. He took a few steps and pulled her along. What could be more important than saving her life?

"My husband cut me off. I have no money. I know this is asking a lot, we just met, but if you could just pay for half of my hotel bill, my friend Sheila could pay the other half. As soon as the hotel finds out about the card, they're going to have a problem." Her face turned white, and a tear slipped out as she explained.

"Don't worry," Connor said, walking into the elevator and closing it before the man caught up with them. "It's not an issue." He patted her shoulder. Right now, her husband cutting off her funds was the least of her problems. "I'll have the hotel put your room on my card."

"Thank you, CJ. I promise I'll pay you back—"

"Don't concern yourself. I have to get something out of my room." While in the elevator, he called the front desk and changed the billing for her room. They stopped briefly in his room, mainly to confuse the man trailing her.

"Where are we going?" she asked as they left his room, walked down the hall, and waited for the elevator.

"For a ride."

They took the elevator down to the lobby, but he didn't step out of the elevator. He turned around and asked for her keycard. "Why?" she asked.

"Just give it to me," he said, waiting as she fumbled in her purse looking for it. She handed it to him, and they took the elevator to her floor, didn't get off, and returned to the lobby again.

"What are we doing?" she asked. "Why are we going up and down in the elevator? I don't get it." She shrugged and tilted her head.

"Never mind. Fun and games. All good," Connor replied, smiling, this time getting off the elevator and walking through the lobby, with Rylee almost running to keep up with him. The man tailing Rylee was nowhere in sight.

"What do you want to talk to me about?" she asked. "And why did you bring your bag? Are you checking out?"

"You ask a lot of questions," he said, smiling. "I thought this might be a good time to seize the day and have an adventure." Before she could ask any more questions, Connor walked her out the front door of the Gaylord. He handed the valet a hundred-dollar bill and the ticket for his car. "Have my car out here within sixty seconds and you'll earn another hundred," he said.

"Yes, sir, right away, sir," the valet replied, then took off, not looking back.

"Thank you for taking care of my hotel bill," she said as he waited for his car.

"I told you it wasn't a problem."

"Are you coming back?"

"Yes, of course. Why don't you come with me? You could have an adventure too." He needed Rylee to go with him but didn't want to frighten her.

"How long would we be gone? I have a session at five-thirty and—"

"Don't worry." He attempted to look reassuring.

Just then, the valet pulled up with his Tesla. "I can't believe this," she said, her eyes growing huge. "I have a Tesla too. Not the S. I have the Y."

"I bet it's red," Connor said, "This is only a rental."

"How did you know I had a red one?" she asked, playfully swatting his arm.

"Get in," he said, opening the passenger's door for her. He didn't tell her he had seen the Tesla card in her wallet. He handed the valet another hundred dollars and popped his bag in the back before getting into the driver's seat.

"Where are we going?" she asked, as she buckled her seatbelt.

"To visit a friend."

As Connor drove, he thought back on the man stalking Rylee. He was sure he'd confused him by taking the elevator to his room, down to the lobby, then back up to her room and down to the entrance again. The guy had no idea they'd even left the hotel. Connor hated not telling Rylee the truth, but discussing things with her would have taken up valuable time.

He drove towards Alexandria, Virginia and Felix. Felix used to work for the CIA. Now he was known in different circles. He was one of the best in the business for making fake identification of any kind. Connor needed a passport and a license for Rylee. He didn't know when he would tell her that he wasn't taking her back to the Gaylord, nor what she would do about it. Should he tell her about her husband putting a hit on her? Should he tell her everything? His occupation? If he did, would she run? He pushed all his questions away and concentrated on his immediate task.

He parked the car several blocks from Felix's place in case the rental company had put any kind of tracker on the vehicle. He'd already sent Felix a text and told him they were stopping by. When the man answered the door, twin four-year-old's held on to each of his ankles, loudly singing a song about sharks, and in his arms he held a four-month-old baby. "I've handled national security for countries worldwide and brought down entire nations, but I can't handle three girls," he laughed. Rylee took the baby from Felix, and the twins dragged Rylee into their bedroom to show her their stuffed animal collection.

Connor explained quietly, "I need some identification so she can travel," motioning to the children's bedroom with his head. He didn't want Rylee overhearing.

"The fastest I can do anything is overnight. I'll take an existing passport and license and put her picture on it," Felix said, pulling a box down from a shelf. "This costs more because they're essentially the real deal. They belonged to the recently departed. Hopefully she doesn't join that club. I'm surprised at you, Connie. I thought your job was the opposite of this—eliminating people, not saving them. Must be softening in your old age." Felix smirked and asked, "You got a picture of her?"

"On my phone." Connor scrolled down, showing Felix. "One more crack about my age and I'll be adding your identification in that box of the departed."

Felix stopped him, pointing at one. "That'll work. Text it. The name on the passport is Anna Antol."

"She might not like it."

"Better than being dead. Stop by in the morning and I'll ensure it's ready. Possibly have it done tonight, but I'd rather you not stop by with the wife at home. She asks a lot of questions."

"The one in there does too." Connor pointed to the bedroom.

"That's how you know they care. If they stop asking questions, they've stopped caring. Maybe I can come up with a reason to go out if you can't wait; run out of milk or bread." Felix smiled. "How does six K sound for both? I guarantee they'll bring no scrutiny from anyone."

"Sounds good. Bitcoin okay?"

"Really? You know cash is king, Connor."

"I need to watch my cash. I'm on the run."

*Ring ring*. Shit. Connor looked down at his phone. Management always found a way to ruin his day. "My bosses. I need to take this," he told Felix.

"Go ahead. I won't stop you," Felix replied, using a utility knife to play with the existing picture on the passport at the kitchen table.

Connor walked out to the front stoop, holding his phone, and pressed ANSWER CALL. Archie's voice blurted, "It's all over the news. Your mark was found this afternoon by housekeeping. They're reporting that the manner of death is undetermined but could be a heart attack. Unfortunately, our new guy isn't working out so well on the other one. He lost the target.

Management wants me to ask if you'd reconsider and take the other job."

"No. I'm heading back."

"You haven't seen her?"

"Who?"

"Rylee Reed. Our man Anthony sent us a picture. It was pretty grainy but she was running with someone, and he looked about your size and build."

"Are you accusing me of something?" Connor had to work hard not to raise his voice.

"Calm down. Just askin' a question."

"Maybe you need to be more careful about the people you hire. Obviously, Anthony doesn't know his job too well if a civilian gave him the slip."

"He's young and motivated and has performed well up to now," Archie said.

"When did you guys ever care about what used to be? I've got to pack." Connor ended the call and re-entered the house. "Morons," he huffed to himself.

"Always good when management takes an interest in their employees, yes?" Felix asked and smirked.

Connor didn't return a smile. "Get that passport done as quick as you can, please."

"I love it when you beg, Connor," Felix said.

* * *

"It's already after five. I'm going to miss my session on creating fatal flaws in my characters," Rylee said, standing on the sidewalk in front of Felix's house.

"What's that?" Connor asked.

"Most literary characters have a trait that leads to their downfall. It may be admirable in some situations, but taken too far..."

"I get it. Like on the one hand, you're trusting of others, but if you're too trusting, you become gullible, and it ends up working against you," he said as they walked towards the car.

She laughed. "TSTL, they call it in romance fiction. 'Too stupid to live.' Another example might be a very passionate man that can't always control it. When he can't, he blows up, lashes out and punches people." She stared and smirked at him.

"Interesting." He didn't return the smile and kept his sunglasses on. "Would you mind if we stopped and ate some pizza or something?"

"Pizza? No. The dough has all kinds of artificial things, and my stomach can't handle cheese. A salad would be good."

Connor grunted and gave her a side-eyed glance. "Your wish is my command," he said, pointing to the sign across the street depicting a salad.

"Perfect, we're already here," she laughed. "But a short visit. I want to get back to my sessions." Connor didn't tell her he wasn't taking her back for any sessions.

As typical with her, it took Rylee ten minutes to look at and eliminate her choices from the menu, then another ten minutes to discuss what she wanted to order with the server. Connor sat patiently, then ordered his pizza and waited for the man to walk away. He couldn't avoid it anymore. He had to ask her. "I have a bold question for you, Rylee." He stared at her pink lips.

"Yes?" she said, swallowing several times, her blue eyes wavering.

"What do you think about coming back to Ireland with me?" Connor searched her eyes for clues and watched her mouth. His palms sweated and he made a list in his head of all the excuses she'd likely come up with not to come, so he'd have an argument ready for each one. Hopefully.

# Chapter 7
# Busting Heads

"The honey is sweet, but the bee has a sting."

— —Benjamin Franklin

"When?" Rylee asked.

"Now, tonight," Connor said.

"I...I'm not sure...I mean, it's crazy. I should drop everything and fly to Ireland with you?"

"What's stopping you?"

"I don't have a passport with me, for one thing, and I'm in the middle of—"

"I've taken care of it. Felix is making one."

"What do you mean, he's making one?"

"That's what he does."

"How does he do that? His house isn't the post office. Is he some master forger or something?" she said with a smile.

"Yes."

She now fully laughed out loud, still not believing him. "Okay,

55

whatever you say. But what about my book? My publisher? My divorce?"

"What about it? That's why they have the internet and phones."

"I don't know. I'm not sure..." She reached for her glass a water, swallowed a mouthful, and then another as if she had to extinguish some internal fire.

Connor said, "I heard you tell your friend you have nothing to go back to. If your life is falling apart, what do you have to lose?" As he poured more water into her glass, he spun more arguments. "It might be good to do something you didn't plan. The other night, you said you wanted to travel. I'm giving you an opportunity."

"I need to think about this. I don't have any money or even my things from the hotel."

"I have money. You won't need to spend a penny. No strings attached. I'll have someone get your things or buy new ones."

"I don't know. This is all so sudden and—"

"I care for you," Connor said, wrapping her hand in his. "We can get to know each other better." Rylee's fingers trembled. Connor's phone vibrated. He let go of Rylee's hand and picked it up, read the text, sent two back. "Your passport's ready. Felix is bringing it over."

"I don't know. Ahh...I need to think about this." She brought her hands to her lap, looking down and pulling her fingers until the server brought their food, which she scarcely touched.

"I promise it will be fun," Connor said. "It could be just the thing you need. You might find inspiration for your next book."

"Maybe. You could be right...I mean, I rarely do things spur of the moment, and I need a change because my life is definitely headed sideways," she replied, staring at Connor. He thought about how she had no idea just how "sideways" it had become—a husband who wanted her dead, a hired assassin already on the way to make it so. He didn't look at her. "Let me just…" She sighed and put her hands in the air. "I'm going to go to the restroom. Give me just a moment." She got up and headed to the back of the restaurant.

Connor knew something was wrong as soon as Felix entered the place a moment later. His face was white, he was blinking too much, and he had no smile, either. His eyes kept darting back and forth, and he'd stopped at the entrance and swiveled his head to look behind, as if someone might have followed. He wouldn't look Connor in the eye, either.

Connor put his hand out for the envelope. Felix placed it in his hand, mouthed, "He has my family," closed his eyes and exhaled.

"Did anyone follow you?" Connor asked, glancing past Felix out the window.

"No. He's back at the house," Felix said. "He has my family gathered in the living room. He's waiting for me to come home. Wants to make sure I deliver the goods." Connor opened the envelope and examined Rylee's new identification before returning them to the envelope and shoving it in his pocket. He looked back at Felix, who whispered behind his hand, "Where is she?"

"In the restroom."

"He plans on showing up at Dulles to kill her. You too, if you're with her. Those are his orders. Before that happens, I imagine he'll kill my entire family and me." He picked up Connor's glass of water and gulped it down. Everyone was drinking his water.

"That won't happen," Connor said, "because I'm going to kill the little twerp first. Just in case he was smart enough to have someone follow you, Rylee and I will go out the back and meet you near your house. Take your time walking home, but don't go in, understand? Wait for us." Felix nodded his head and headed towards the door.

Rylee returned from the bathroom just as Felix departed.

"What's going on? I thought I saw Felix leave." Rylee pointed at the door swinging closed.

"He did. Sit down. I have a problem. I'll explain." After she sat, Connor continued, "Some men are after me, and they've threatened Felix and his family. I have to go back to his house and deal with it."

"Why are they after you?" she asked in a panic, her eyebrows raised.

"The business I'm in."

"What kind of business?"

"I'm an assassin."

Rylee's eyes widened. She shook her head and bolted, not waiting to hear more. She ran towards the back of the restaurant, through the swinging doors, and into the kitchen. Connor opened his wallet, dumped some money on the table, picked up her coat, and followed. When he exited the back door of the shop, she was gone. He'd lost both her trust and her just that quickly.

*　*　*

When Connor arrived on Felix's block, the man came out from behind a parked car where he'd been hiding and asked with trembling lips, "Where's Rylee?"

"She took off," Connor said.

"I don't blame her. He still has my family under gunpoint in the living room. I peeked through a window."

"Is the back door open or locked?"

"Locked, most likely."

"Have a key? I need to get in the back door quickly, while you go in the front."

"Sure," Felix said, passing it to him. "I'll use the key hidden under the flowerpot on the front porch to get in. What are you going to do?"

"Keep him occupied," Connor said, as he pulled out an enormous gun from inside his jacket. "And you can help." He passed Felix a smaller handgun from his boot.

"I haven't fired a weapon in years," Felix said, his voice rising, holding the gun away from himself. "What if I hit one of my children or my wife?"

"Don't take the safety off. Just draw his attention and I'll do all the shooting."

"The guy might retaliate and shoot my family."

"He could shoot them anyway, even if you aren't holding a weapon. More likely he won't shoot them if he thinks you might shoot *him*. Trust me. I've got this. I'm going to take this guy down before he can do a bloody thing."

Connor heard a noise and turned, his gun out and ready to fire. It was Rylee. "What can I do to help?" she asked, not making eye contact with Connor but looking at Felix. Connor noticed her hands shaking.

"You want to help?" Connor asked, staring at her.

"I don't want anything to happen to the children," she said, closing her eyes and taking a calming breath.

Felix said, "That's probably not a good idea, since this guy is after—"

"Stay outside," Connor interrupted, flashing a warning look at Felix. He passed Rylee the phone. "When we leave, count to twenty-five and hit redial. The number belongs to Felix. The ring will be our signal. Once we hear the phone ring inside, we'll both come through the front and back doors at the same time. The guy's mind will be on overload. Let's roll."

"Wait a minute," she said, looking at me. "What did Felix mean that it wasn't a good idea for me to help?" She stared at Connor.

"It's nothing. We don't have time for questions right now."

"Can you just shoot him in the arm or leg?" she asked.

"No. I can't take the chance of him shooting Felix or his family."

Rylee nodded and held the phone while Felix headed to the front, and he headed towards the back.

A moment later, Connor heard the familiar *Ring, ring, ring, ring.* On cue, he pushed through the door of the kitchen. *Crack!* The door slammed against the wall. He hurried to the living room, where a man sat, immediately beginning to stand and saying, "What the fuck do you think you're—"

Connor fired, not letting the man complete his question or get off a shot. The bullet flashed and left the muzzle. It hit the man in the middle of his forehead. The hired gun slid to the ground in his tailored suit and landed on his back, his head turned to one side. The gun fell from his hand, and a small hole appeared in his head. A drop of blood dripped down his nose and cheek until it began flowing faster, finally pooling underneath his head. A foul smell, like urine mixed with smoke, filled the air. Felix's wife screamed as she pulled her baby closer to her chest. The twins ran across the room with open-mouthed and -eyed expressions and latched onto Felix's leg. Felix handed his smaller weapon back to Connor and scooped the girls up, taking them to their bedroom as his wife followed.

Moments later, there was a tapping at the back door. Connor lifted the roller blind and saw Rylee. "It's over," he said as he opened the door and escorted her in. She had surprised him again; she hadn't run away like he thought she might as soon as she did her part of the job.

"Is everyone okay?" Rylee asked as she tilted her head and touched his shoulder.

"Everyone but him," Connor said, pointing to the assassin dead on the floor. "If you don't mind, I'll give you the details later. I need to wrap things up and get the body out of here. This isn't good for Felix's wife and children. It's not good for you, either. Wait in the other room with them."

Rylee stared at the dead man. "There wasn't any other way? He doesn't look like a killer."

"Murder has been around since the beginning of time. He threatened Felix and his family. I didn't have a choice in the matter." He removed the tablecloth, laid it down on the floor, and rolled the body on it.

"The fifth commandment says we shouldn't kill," Rylee said.

"People kill in the name of God all the time in the Bible. Hypocritical to say never kill under any circumstances. I didn't take an innocent life here, no matter how helpless he appears now, lifeless and without his weapon. In this case, killing him was justifiable. I was defending myself and protecting them." He wrapped the cloth around the body and tied it securely with twine he'd found in one of the kitchen drawers. He placed a trash bag over the guy's head and then another, then wrapped the cover around the body. Normally, it wasn't his responsibility to get rid of the body. He took more garbage bags, cut them apart and wrapped them around the corpse.

He looked up and noticed Rylee had never left, but was instead studying him, a pained stare on her face, clenching her fists. "Is there more to this?" she asked.

"I don't know what you mean. I need to pull the car in the drive before I take this out."

"Before when you interrupted Felix and he said—"

"I need to get the body out of here. Monitor things until I return."

"What does that entail, exactly?"

"If the police come, get rid of them."

"What? Why would they come?"

"Neighbors may have heard or seen something suspicious and reported it."

"Your gun had a silencer." She pointed at the bulge in his jacket.

"The wife did some screaming and strange people entered the property," he said.

"You mean him?" Rylee pointed at the dead man.

"And us. Stop asking questions. I've got to move the car closer."

"But what should I say if the cops—"

"Yer a writer. Spin a yarn." He gave her a twisted smile and walked out the door.

Connor should have told Rylee the truth about everything. She should know a hired killer is hunting her because her husband wants her dead, and Connor might fail to protect her, and she'd die. But instead, Connor kept his mouth shut and her unaware. He'd failed before. It seemed he was a competent killer but not adept at protecting the people he loved. Why?

If he told her everything, she wouldn't stay with the likes of him, someone his Father once called a coward. As it was, Connor would have a hard time getting Rylee to go on the plane with him. If he told her all of it, she wouldn't come—she would run, and he would have lost everything, his job, and any chance to get to know Rylee Reed. *I'll be alone.* Connor gripped and turned the wheel as he checked his mirrors and backed the vehicle into the driveway at Felix's house.

Her mind raced as CJ drove. "How often have you done this?" she asked. Was she now officially a co-conspirator in a deadly crime?

She imagined the prosecuting attorney would likely call her an accessory.

CJ looked at her quickly and asked, "Do you really want the answer?" Then he looked back at the road again.

"I do." *I think.* This was like a car wreck; she wanted to see, but turned away when she got to the scene, afraid to take in the horror.

"I'll tell you everything you want to know another time," he said, his voice soft and his gaze alert.

*What does he mean by everything?* "Where are we?" she asked.

CJ gave her a side-eyed glance, drawing his breath in slowly and letting it out again, like she often did when someone wanted something from her while she was writing. *Would he kill me if I keep asking questions?* "Rock Creek Park," he said, pulling the Tesla off onto a service road. The car bounced as he crossed a stone bridge. A sign read in sizeable red letters, "Do Not Enter, Road Closed for Repair."

"What about the road?" Rylee pointed to the sign.

"Don't worry." He gently patted her leg. "'Tis be alright." She wondered if he deliberately used his Irish accent whenever he wanted to distract her and get her to go along with him. David had another approach—he yelled and badgered.

Connor drove until they reached an area that looked smooth enough to pull off, levelled with smooth stone, then parked behind a group of trees and turned the lights off. "Wait here," he said as he unsnapped his seatbelt.

"By myself?"

"Unless you want me to leave the dead guy here to keep you company while I dig the hole."

"Don't be a sarcastic shit," she testily replied, shooting him a look.

CJ exited the vehicle, went to the trunk, opened it, and pulled the body out. She heard it hit the ground with a clunk, then listened to more scraping sounds as he dragged it across the gravel. The moonlight framed CJ's hunched silhouette as he moved the body and a small shovel up a hill until he disappeared into the forest. Rylee brought her head down on her lap, chewed the inside of her cheek, and rocked back and forth in her seat. She removed her phone from her purse and checked her messages, anything to keep her mind off what had happened and was still happening. How does one get rid of a body? She looked it up on Google. The advice was to bury it deep so animals couldn't dig it up. The surrounding trees closed in, and the smell of pine came through the open window. She shouldn't have searched for something like that, she realized, shutting the phone off. Law enforcement could use your phone searches against you.

The only light came from a quarter moon and the interior lamp of the Tesla. The hoot of an owl called out, and she thought she heard someone breathing. Turning around, she'd discovered no one there. She tried saying affirmations. "I'm a good person. I'm a good person. I'm a good person," she chanted, wrapping her arms around herself. *Who is with someone burying a body right now. Geez.* How did she get into this mess? She married the wrong man twenty-five years ago, and now she's with one who... She brought her fingers to her lips to make herself quiet and started biting her nails. She had finally broken herself of that habit years ago, but here she was doing it again. What if the park police came? They were down a closed road. The cops would want to know why she was here. What could she tell them? She's waiting for her friend to bury a body...no. She's conducting research for her novel, that's it! This is starting to become just like it is with David, only now she was coming up with excuses for CJ instead. What if the police checked her phone and saw her search history? She couldn't even be an accessory to a crime the right way. Damn.

One hour later, CJ's silhouette appeared. It felt like a whole day and night had gone by. He threw the shovel in the trunk and walked around to the driver's side and climbed in. "It's taken care of. Not as deep as I usually go, but deep enough and far back enough in the woods. It should pose no problem."

"Good to know you're an expert at burying bodies. I'll be sure and tell my girlfriends," she said, all her nervousness flying out of her in a barrage of words.

"Who's being sarcastic now?" A relaxed smile spread across CJ's face.

# Chapter 8
# Honey & Sweet Things

Saturday

This made no sense. She had agreed to fly to Ireland with a hit man. CJ purchased tickets for the first flight out—two a.m., flight #729, non-stop to Dublin. Rylee had officially joined the TSTL (Too Stupid To Live) group. Members of her romance writing group always chided each other and snickered about them; the kind of lead female character who threw caution to the wind, walked down dark alleys at night, ran out of gasoline and then asked a serial killer for help, or now like her, agreed to go on a road trip with a hitman. She rubbed her eyes and sighed.

"Ladies and gentlemen, on behalf of the crew," the pilot announced, "I ask that you please direct your attention to the screens above as air personnel review emergency procedures." Her heart pounded in her chest faster. All she had to do was get up and leave, but as she clutched her seatbelt to remove it, one of the crew members armed the door, moving a lever and locking it in place with a giant metal pin. Then the plane began backing up from the terminal. It was too late.

The other crew members continued pointing at screens and emergency exits as if they were playing a game of charades. She looked at the televisions and thought about her favorite crime shows, the ones about women who hook up with evil men and end up breaking the law, on the run from the authorities. She imagined herself featured. "Shut it off, please," she said, and squeezed her eyes closed, twisting her fingers.

She'd failed again—had picked another man who didn't tell the truth, who wasn't real. How could she trust him? How could she trust herself? According to Felix, Connor hadn't hesitated in killing the man in his house. Connor told her himself that killing was justifiable. His ability to kill, his matter-of-fact behavior in doing so and seemingly not to experience any remorse horrified her. His methodical actions as he wrapped and got rid of the body left her reeling. Rylee believed it was God's responsibility to repay evil, not Connor's.

She was an idiot for letting Connor talk her into this, but Felix had encouraged her to go with him: "You can't go back to the hotel or anywhere else you've been before." Felix didn't provide her with further details. *Connor said I'm gullible. He's right.* In eight hours they'll land, and she'll be on his turf. She bit her cuticle. Why did she go with him? What was she thinking? She couldn't even distract her mind with her phone because he'd thrown it out the window of the car on the way to Dulles, afraid they could track him through her. How did Connor's problem with his bosses become hers?

"What's wrong?" Connor asked. She jumped and twisted in her seat. She couldn't find the softness of his eyes. His shades shielded them. Who wears sunglasses when it's pitch black out? "I thought you'd like business class. You've gone quiet. And all the fidgeting, what's up?" *Is he just using me to get away?*

"It's nice. I'm a nervous traveler." Part of it was true. *I'm very nervous about him.*

* * *

Connor had been surprised and happy when Rylee still agreed to come to Ireland with him even after the kill, but he'd worked hard to scare her. He had told her that if anyone had seen her with him, they'd attempt to get information out of her. He used the word "torture" and warned, "Yer life's in danger now. You're safer with me. I can protect ya. Come with me until I figure things out." Her face had turned white, and she couldn't get her words out, but shook her head yes, agreeing to come.

The false identification caused no problems, just as Felix said. It was as good as the real thing because it was the real thing, and in eight hours they'd land in his country and he'd finally have the advantage. He felt bad about lying to her, but part of what he'd told her was the truth. Her life *was* in danger, but not because of Connor. "Is the seat not comfortable?" he asked.

"Yes, it's great." She twisted her hands in her lap, not looking in his direction, eying the emergency exit. She acted afraid of him. There was a distance between them now that hadn't been there before, and it bothered Connor.

"Try to sleep. It's a long trip and we don't know what we'll find on the other end when we land. We need to be rested."

She turned away and look out the window as the plane taxied down the runway.

"I need to ask you something, CJ." She faced him as the plane picked up speed.

"My first name's Connor," he said as the aircraft lifted from the ground.

"That's a nice name. Like I said, I need to ask you something, CJ." Her hands gripped the armrests.

Here we go. Rylee always had to dig down and understand things. "Yes," Connor said, opening one eye, attempting a friendly face. Probably impossible. Connor hadn't been a nice guy since his mother's death. Hopefully, he didn't scare Rylee.

"Hmmm. Isn't there a rule about killing another hit man? Won't they kick you out of the Assassination Association?"

Good one. Assassination Association. Connor held back his smile. He liked the way her mind worked. "Don't worry about it."

"Is that your answer for everything?" She shook her head at him and then glanced out the window into blackness.

"Pretty much. If I do become worried about anyone, I remove them. Let's see how this plays out. If it's a problem, I'll take care of it. Now, please, rest." He removed his sunglasses, lowered the overhead lights, and closed his eyes.

*Crap. Did he threaten me?* He sounded like David, but David always meant he'd take someone to court and sue their asses. He didn't mean he was going to kill anyone, at least not on purpose. *Is Connor going to kill me?* "You said I'd be safer with you, but I don't see how."

"It should be obvious. Go to sleep." CJ pushed his seat back to align with hers. Business class did have comfortable seats, she had to admit. His long fingers wrapped around hers and he gave a gentle squeeze. Rylee wondered, was he holding her hand so she couldn't leave his side? He leaned over, his warm breath hitting her ear, and whispered, "I've waited a long time to meet my queen," his eyes closing. Queen? What did he mean by that? At least Connor revealed who he was right away, not like her soon to be ex-husband. *Yes, Rylee, so comforting to know he's a hitman.* She swallowed several times to keep from either laughing or crying, she wasn't sure.

Rylee's eyes popped open, and she turned her head and gazed out the window again. It was black outside, and she could only see the lights coming from the plane's body. She must have fallen asleep for a few minutes. She leaned her head against the window. The crew had dimmed all the interior lights. Everyone on the plane seemed to settle down, and all the voices in the cabin disappeared over the next half-hour. Soon there was nothing but a muffled cry from a baby near the back of the aircraft, the engine's hum, and her mind shuffling and repeating all her questions and fears. She couldn't sleep. There was a divider between the seats, but he got as close to her as he could and reached across and slowly unbuttoned her blouse. Rylee's breathing slowed at first as she held her breath. *Do I want him to stop or keep going?* And then her breathing quickened as he pushed her bra up and touched her breasts, massaging and squeezing them. He stretched over, bringing his mouth to them, hovered, then zeroed in, placing his lips on her nipple, sucking it, swirling it in his mouth. Her body trembled and her clit throbbed. *What if someone sees?* One of his hands came to the top of her head and pulled the clip holding her bun in place. Her hair burst free, and strands fell away and around her. "Your hair smells like honey," he sang, lifting his head.

She moved in her seat. "I like honey," she replied, squirming against his touch.

"Me too. I like sweet things." He ran his fingers up to her lips. "They're hard to find in this world." She could feel his eyes on her in the dark.

"I can't do this," she whispered. She was too bashful to become part of any Mile High Club, and had never had secret sex in a public space. David didn't even like to hold hands in public.

"You don't have to do anything. Let me do it," he whispered, bringing his fingers down to her neck and then her arms, his fingertips lingering and writing imaginary words on her skin. Their eyes met in the dark. "Spread your legs," he said with a throaty voice.

"No, I have a better idea," Rylee said.

"What's that, my lovely?" he asked, curiosity taking hold.

# Chapter 9
# Master John Goodfellow

"It is the honey in my veins that makes my
blood thicker, and my soul quieter."

———Friedrich Nietzsche

"Unzip your... um... pants," Rylee said.

Connor chuckled, "Are you sure?" It could be she was teasing him.

"No, it's your turn and I... just do it," she said.

"I have an idea how to make this better." Connor stood up and squeezed into her seat with her. He pushed the seat all the way back, allowing them to lie down next to one another. He unbuttoned and unzipped his pants and brought her hand to the opening. "The club is open for business," and chuckled. Rylee hesitated and Connor said, "Forgive my manners, a formal introduction is definitely required." He grasped her hand and brought it inside his pants. "This is Rylee, and Rylee, this is Master John Goodfellow," and moved his cock outside his pants, bringing his hand wrapped around her hand along with it. He moved her hand up and down his cock. "I think he's taken a shine to you already." She snickered and his cock grew under her touch. "Don't be afraid of him, he's easygoing and doesn't mind a bit of thrashing, squeezing her hand tighter around his cock and bringing it down and up again. "There you go," he sighed as he removed his hand from hers. "I'll let you two get acquainted." She picked up the pace and experimented. She brought her hand down the length of him and then came back up and stopped at the head, working that part alone, using her fingers to flick it. His erection had grown and a bit of pre-cum had moistened her hands. He stared at her face. The cabin light caught her lips, they were framed in the light—so, so pink. Connor wanted their velvet softness on him. "Come girl, put yer head in my lap, give Master John Goodfellow yer sweet soft lips. Kiss him." Her eyes wavered for a few seconds, but she opened her mouth in anticipation. Connor knew then she'd comply. Rylee scooted down lower in the seat, putting her knees on the floor, between his legs. Her mouth touched him, hesitantly at first, licking just the tip and then longer laps down the head, and eventually she took more and more of him, while she used her hand to follow her mouth, coming up the length of his shaft. Every so often, she'd swirl her tongue around the foreskin or latch onto his balls and caress them. Connor felt like laughing or calling out, but couldn't, not in the belly of a plane, full of people at night. He reached over and took his jacket from his seat and covered her head and his lap, shielding her and keep prying eyes at bay. She all but disappeared under the covering and with every mouthful she brought him closer and closer to cuming. He wound her hair around his hand, made a fist and began directing her head where he wanted her to be and at the speed he desired. His other hand was underneath, at her breast and he played with her nipple, squeezing it in rhythm with her movements on his cock until the nipple became hard, like a small pebble. He heard her breathing come faster and little gasps escaped as his cock grew larger and he thrust it down her throat deeper and faster. Rylee kept up with him, so he didn't lessen his fervor. "Good girl, take all of it," he called, pushing deep into her throat. Finally, with one thrust, his cock spasmed, he squeezed her nipple and held her head to his cock, encouraging her to swallow all of it. Rylee's mouth sucked and squeezed and then swallowed every drop. "Lovely, Rylee, loveleeeeee, leeee," he whispered, loosening his hold on her. She licked his cock clean and gently placed Master John Goodfellow back in his pants and sat up. Her eyes were fiery in the light, glints of color coming off them, but he couldn't figure out from where. Connor brought her to him, sliding her from the floor until she was on top of him. He kissed her deeply, "Thank you, sweet girl," and watched as she pushed herself away, relaxed into her side of the seat, laid her head against the window and closed her eyes. Connor returned to his own seat and rearranged his coat to cover her. He didn't remember drifting away, only that his heart felt full and his mind was peaceful in a way it hadn't been before.

Connor's phone vibrated. He'd slept for five hours. She'd come back to him; he thought as he held her hand. He grabbed his phone with his free one and looked at the text. It was from Archie.

You made a mistake. 1chance 2fix

24hrs to X target

call when done.

Connor turned the phone off and slipped the cell back in his pocket. Archie was right. Connor only had one chance to fix his life and having Rylee in it was the answer. The lights inside the plane were off and it was peaceful. The only noise came from a few snoring passengers and the engines. The plane flew well above the clouds as the sun rose, giving the sky a pink glow. Connor looked down at Rylee as he held her hand. She'd removed her glasses. He suspected Rylee hid behind them. She wasn't like some women who flaunted what they had. Rylee hid her beauty away, waiting for someone to discover it, or maybe someone worth sharing it with.

Her eyes sprung open, connecting with his. "What are you doing?" She asked.

"Nothing."

"You were staring at me."

"No. Just checking if you were awake," taking his hand, brushing her hair away from her eyes.

"Liar," she shouted.

"Maybe I was staring," Connor confessed. "What if I was?"

"Why?" she asked and gazed at him with focus.

"Because you're beautiful." He made her blush, and she pulled her hand away.

"You are Irish, aren't you? Full of the blarney," And then she rolled her eyes and swatted Connor's arm.

* * *

"How long a drive to your house?" Rylee asked as he drove his car out of the long-term parking area of the Dublin Airport.

"Almost two hours, but I should warn you, it's small, more a cottage." He patted her leg, "I enjoyed our episode on the flight," and glanced at Rylee.

"Ahh, me too," she said and blushed. "I've never done anything like that before... you know, out in the open like that," a smile spreading.

"It excited you then?"

"Yes," her eyes resting on him.

"I liked it too. Makes the blood race. We can do something like

74

that again." Connor beamed when Rylee said the experience of being discovered by others excited her. Connor had thought he would have had to take control, that she'd be too timid. Her blow job was a game changer.

"Your car is nice. I knew it would be black," she said, interrupting his thoughts of this morning. "This isn't an S, though."

"No. It's a Plaid," he said.

"La-de-da," and flipped her hand back and forth, laughing. "How fast do you go, two hundred miles an hour?"

"On some of these roads, I can," smiling back at her.

"What town do you live in?"

"It's more rural, but it's called West Connemara. I can see the ocean from my house and there's plenty of space for my bees and—"

"I can't wait to see the bees," she said.

It was raining again, he flicked the wipers on and the water floated off the window allowing him to see the beauty of Ireland, the lush green fields, mixed in with hard, large rocks that had been here forever. Permanence, something that lasted. That's what he wished he had, someone or something that wouldn't leave him. He'd given up on that desire after his mother passed and then his eyes traveled to Rylee and back at the rocks and the road again.

"It's kind of strange you picked a place to live so far away from the airport, with what you do," she said.

"How so?" Connor asked.

"A two-hour drive every time you come home and leave—it's time consuming."

"I don't see it that way. It's a way to decompress and gives me time to return to my real world and self. I can fly from Cork if I need to. That airports closer to my cottage, but there's less choice in flights."

"What will you do if they fire you? Work for someone else or change careers?"

"Retire. I have enough money saved and I have my bee's."

"Do they let you retire?" She asked, a shadow seemed to fall over her face.

"The bees don't care. Unless something happens to them, they get mites, or the queen dies and they don't make a new one, they keep doing their thing." She wrinkled her nose, cocked her head, and squinted at him. "Oh, you're talking about my employer. Hopefully, they won't have a problem once they calm down about what's transpired." Connor knew they wouldn't calm down and any retirement would come with a death sentence, but he wouldn't worry Rylee about it.

"Sounds like you have it all figured out. Are you going to tell me how you got into this?

"Into what, the beekeeping?"

"No, the killing thing," her foot shaking back and forth.

"Do I have to?"

"I need to know." Her face was all business, lips pursed, hands in her lap and eyes thoughtful.

Connor sighed, he took a breath of air and exhaled and gave her what she wanted, the answer. "I had a respectable job once, maybe not by your standards. I ran numbers for a bloke. I was only nineteen and did okay with it. Still lived at home with Mum. Her health wasn't good, she had emphysema and I took care of her. One day I come home, and I found her on the floor, beaten. A couple of smack addicts had robbed her. They stomped her because she wouldn't give them her grocery money. She died a couple weeks later. I hunted them down, followed them, learned their schedules and, when the time was right, finished them both. They were the first two. It doesn't take long for word to spread. The coppers interrogated me, but they couldn't prove anything. A couple of months later, while I was getting soused at a bar I favored, a man reached out. He sobered me up and gave me a stiff talking to. Said I showed aptitude and there was a place for me, but I needed to stay out of the bars. He partnered me up with a by the book kind of guy who taught me the ropes. About a year later, I went solo. Been working for them ever since." He took his eyes off the road once or twice to see how she was taking it. Her face displayed no reaction. Connor knew he was taking a chance confiding in her. Pally would have shot him dead and her too, for knowing what she knew.

"Do you ever feel bad about it?" Connor knew what she wanted to hear, but he couldn't give her the answer she desired. "Only once. The rest of the time, they were all deserving of what they got. The world is a better place without them." He watched her face. Her body stiffened. She opened her mouth to say something and then stopped and said nothing for a minute. He didn't tell Rylee that *she was the one time* he'd felt bad, so bad he became disloyal.

"What about the beekeeping, why that?" Rylee asked.

Connor could see his white cottage framed by the ocean, surrounded by acres of green land and his goats in the pasture coming into view. Maggie must have let them out. He paid her to take care of things. "We're here. I'll tell you about it later," Connor said, and pulled the car up the long drive. He saw Clover with her tail in the air, standing outside the front door. *Why is she out?*

"It's breathtaking," Rylee said. Her eyes danced, and she unsnapped her seatbelt excitedly before he brought the car to a stop. Connor wanted to caution her about waiting until he checked for trouble but before he knew it, she was outside the car. Connor followed briskly, and stepped in front of Rylee, arriving at the front of the house first. Clover meandered down the steps, rubbed against his leg and then Rylee's. She bent down to pet Clover, and as she did, Connor noticed the front door wasn't closed all the way. He couldn't imagine Maggie doing that. She viewed every breathing person as a probable enemy. Connor grabbed Rylee's arm and walked her to the side of the house and drew his weapon. He'd wisely unpacked it from its special case as soon as they'd left the confines of the airport and slipped it inside his coat.

"Wait here," Connor said. "I'm going to check the inside. Normally the door's locked and today it's not." Rylee nodded her head, and her face changed to worry. Connor crept towards the house with his arm stretched out in front of him, clutching his gun. Connor pushed the door with his foot and it squeaked as it swung open. Shadows hung on the white stucco walls and a beam of sunlight caressed the painting on the wall, a landscape of a field of lavender, impasto strokes of shades of pinks and purples high-lighted against a cerulean sky. It was the first thing Connor purchased from a paid hit. He tried to buy something special for the cottage after each gig, usually art or an antique. He loved his cottage at this time of day and usually he'd be drinking a cup of Barry's tea, followed by a pint by now. Would this be his last thought? It would be if he didn't keep his guard up. He had an intense thirst, and his stomach churned. Had someone violated the safety of his home?

Nothing seemed out of place. No drawers were open, and the bowl of apples on the table still held five. The sink was empty and nothing was on the counters. The small bathroom in the hall was empty, the bathtub held no one, and the toilet paper roll looked to be the same size.

Connor approached his small bedroom, slid the pocket door open, and scanned the locks on the windows; they were still in the down position. The closet was open and held only his clothes. The bed was exactly as he left it, the white sheets crisp, with no inden-tation in the pillow. His mother's quilt still lay at the bottom of the bed, folded exactly the way he'd left it. He remembered when she made it, using their old clothes to create the squares. 'It's called a crazy quilt, son. Ain't it gay? Imagine the parties you'll dream of with this covering you.' He never dreamed of any parties, but it comforted him when he covered himself at night, remembering how she sat by the fire in their small row home in Dublin, sewing the quilt by hand night after night by the fire and singing her old Irish songs. He missed her songs and laughter; it was nothing but quiet here. He returned to the living room and left the house.

"Did you find anything?" Rylee asked, touching his arm. Connor shook his head no, "All clear," he said, pulling away and waved his hand to follow him.

# Chapter 10
# Superhuman

"The bee collects honey from flowers in
such a way as to do the least damage or
destruction to them, and he leaves
them whole, undamaged and fresh,
just as he found them."

— —Saint Francis de Sales

Rylee hadn't expected this. CJ wore expensive clothes and drove a luxury automobile. This house revealed a different side of him. Original landscape paintings adorned the walls, and an antique curio cabinet with beveled glass held china in the kitchen. A fieldstone fireplace was centered on one wall, with two comfortable chairs and a small couch arranged in front of it. *I want to live like this—with a minimum of things, each of them unique.*

The kitchen was small but lovely, with white quartz counters. The floors were old distressed wide pine planks. The cottage was like a small jewel. *Maybe CJ was right. I won't want to leave.*

"What do you think?" CJ asked as he came closer and picked up her hand.

"I love it. When can I see the bees?"

"Something to drink first, and if there's enough light, we'll walk the property and I'll show you the hives. If it's too dark, we'll save it for tomorrow." CJ brought her towards his chest and wrapped his arms around her.

"I'd like tea. Should I prepare it?" Rylee asked, gazing up at him.

"I'd rather you put your feet up. You didn't sleep much on the plane. You need to chill. I'll fix a pot. Would you like it with honey or sugar or plain?"

"Honey, please. From your bees, I hope."

"For sure. An even exchange, then; your honey for some of mine." CJ kissed her lips gently, then moved to the kitchen. "You can have your tea on the back porch if you like. It's not too nippy yet and we can watch the sun go down."

"That sounds wonderful. What am I going to do without my things?" she asked, turning to him.

"I can take you to Clifden. It's only about nine kilometers away. I'll buy whatever you need. Can you wait until morning?"

"I guess. I'll borrow one of your shirts and wash my things in the sink, or maybe you have a washer and dryer?"

"Voila," CJ said, opening a cabinet by the sink. "I have a small unit. The washer and dryer are all in one. But I'm going to enjoy seeing you in one of my shirts." He smiled.

The kettle whistled. CJ removed it from its flame, waited a minute or two before pouring the water from it into the teapot, and swirled the tea bags around. He placed the pot, two cups on their saucers, and the honey on the tray. He added a plate with some kind of cookies.

"What are those?" she asked, pointing at the plate.

"Biscuits to go with tea."

"What are the ingredients?" *Hopefully, its nothing bad.*

"I don't know exactly."

"Could you check?"

"Sure." He placed the tray back on the table, then opened the cabinet, took the package down, and passed it to her. "Good to go?" he asked as she read.

"Mmm, maybe one would be alright." *Crap, it has wheat and palm oil, but I don't want to be rude.*

"You certainly police yourself."

"I'm sorry. I just—"

"Don't apologize. It's great that you care about what goes in your body. I should take better care of myself." Patting his stomach, CJ picked up the tray. "Let's go enjoy what's left of the day."

Going outside, she said, "Oh yes, I see the hives over there. Eight—that's a lot. I didn't know bees liked sunlight. For some reason I thought hives would be kept in the shade."

CJ placed the tray down and poured the tea into their cups. "I'll let you add your own honey. Bees like a little shade, but you have less disease if you keep your hives in the sun. They get a dappling of shade from those trees over there, plus they're protected from the wind. There's a small stream behind the trees where they can get water, and then all the wildflowers that grow naturally provide the ideal location to gather."

"You've thought of everything for them." She used the honey dipper to drip the honey into her cup. She put a little bit of onto her spoon and brought it to her lips. It tasted like heaven, and she licked the spoon clean. Local honey was good for allergies and there were no preservatives in this.

I think you missed some," CJ said as he ran his finger over her lips and brought it to his own mouth and licked his finger. "If you take care of them, they'll take care of you and make honey. I'll take those extra calories for you."

"It's not the calories I'm worried about. Unhealthy ingredients in food can kill you," she explained, stopping. CJ sat down next to her and grabbed for her hand, making it tremble. Then he stood and brought her with him. The scent of his hair, tea, honey, and the sea swam in her nose. Some nearby birds made magical music as they ate from a feeder he had hung from the porch. "I missed some," he said, and came in closer still, placing his lips on top of hers and kissing her.

"What kind of birds are those?" she asked with CJ's arms wrapped around her. "They sound so pretty."

"Skylarks," CJ said.

Just as Rylee relaxed, she saw movement from the corner of her eye. A man holding something ducked down by the tall grasses by a white barn directly across from the porch. She buried her head in CJ's chest, acted like she hadn't seen the man, and spoke into his chest instead. "A man is hiding by the building over there, but he doesn't know I saw him."

CJ nodded, bent down and kissed her, pretending he hadn't heard her. He walked her body backward, pressed her to the side of the house, and slid his hand under her shirt. "We have to make this look realistic. I apologize if this isn't what you want right now." He then dipped his tongue in her mouth, bringing his hand to her breast and kneading it. "We must make him believe we're taking this inside and into the bedroom. He'll come for us. Understand?"

She nodded, and CJ separated her legs with one of his. He pushed against her pelvis with his swollen member. That much was very real. "Come," he said after a minute of kissing and staring into her eyes. "Don't be frightened." He led Rylee into the house. He stopped in the kitchen, removed a knife from the woodblock, and handed it to her. "Take this, just in case." He placed the knife block with the missing knife under the sink cabinet. He then removed a bottle of whiskey and two glasses from the cabinet, poured half of it down the drain, poured a little in each glass, and set them and the bottle down on the table. It appeared like two people had been drinking quite a lot. He walked over to his coat hanging on the chair, removed his gun, then turned all the lights in the house off. He led her into the bedroom. "Lay on the bed. Hand me your glasses and spread your hair across the pillow."

"Can't I keep my glasses?" she asked.

"Who sleeps with their glasses on?" He waited for her to pass them. "I'm going to arrange some towels and other clothing to make it look like I'm in bed with you." After he was done, he took the quilt at the end of the bed and threw it on top of her.

"Convincing," she said, looking down at the scene. "How long do you think he'll wait before trying anything?"

"Good question. Some like to take you out while you're in the middle of the act and others want to wait until yer done. They feel better about sending you out with a smile on your face. We'll have to wait and see how this guy flies."

"Where will you be?"

"In that partially opened closet, right there. Don't worry, I'll protect you," CJ said, walking over and standing in front of it. "It's almost dark now. From this point on, I think it best we don't converse."

Rylee wanted to cry but didn't want to distract CJ. She put her hands over her mouth to hold everything in and whispered, *please, God, protect me and CJ.* She squeezed her eyes closed, and as the tears came, she recycled her thoughts. *Would CJ shoot me by mistake? Why did I go with him?* She took a deep breath, exhaled every once in a while, and tried to calm herself. She was afraid to move and check the time on the clock on the bedside table. Had she been in bed fifteen minutes, an hour, or two? The *tick, tick, tick* of the clock drove her crazy. Suddenly a sound—*meow.* It was only Clover. The cat circled the bed, jumped up, landed on her feet, climbed towards the top, and nestled near her pillow. Rylee wanted to hide; she didn't want to be a target for an assassin.

*Squeak.* The back door opened. Rylee opened her eyes and

saw Clover's head come up from resting on its paws. Its eyes shone in the dark, and it looked towards the entryway. Rylee didn't move her head. She froze in place as steps moved inside the room. But Clover didn't and jumped off the bed onto the floor. That's when all hell broke loose. The attacker stumbled. There was grunting and groaning, men wrestling, and the sound of something, possibly metal, hitting the floor. Was it someone's gun? She jumped from the mattress and joined the fray, wrapping her arms around the shorter man's neck while still holding the knife CJ had given her. She pretended she was riding a bucking bronco and climbed up further on the intruder's back as he tried to fling her off. The attacker held something in his hand, and as he brought it up, she brought her knife down on the attacker's back, causing the man to drop his weapon. After she gouged the assassin many times, the man stopped twirling and fell to the ground with her on top of him.

She continued her attack, sitting on him and screaming until she felt CJ's hand on her wrist and heard his voice. "You're safe now. He's not a threat." He turned on the light, removed the weapon from her hand, and threw it across the room. Connor scooped her up and held her, walking her into the bathroom while she looked back at the man on the floor. He cleaned her hands and face of blood and made her exchange her blood-splattered shirt for a new one while keeping an eye on the man, who wasn't moving. He brought her into the living room, handed her a half-filled glass of whiskey, and made her drink it. Connor returned to the bedroom with trash bags and closed the door. *He doesn't want me to see what's coming next.*

Sunday

Rylee never thought she would be capable of killing anyone, but now she knew the truth. She could kill. CJ removed the body from the bedroom and was gone for hours, hours she spent crying and replaying what had happened.

She heard something outside and checked the window. CJ was back. "We have to talk," he said after walking through the door.

"Where did you bury the body?" she asked.

"Far from here. Don't think about it. I have to be straight with you." He sat down on the chair as she sat on the couch across from him and wrapped herself in a blanket.

She leaned forward. "What about?" she asked. *What bomb will he drop this time?*

"I said people were trying to kill me. The truth is, that's a lie."

She didn't know what to say, but realized if they weren't trying to kill CJ... "Who then?" They were after someone. She searched CJ's eyes for answers.

"It's you. Someone wants to kill you," CJ said, pointing his finger at her.

"Me? Why? Who?" CJ looked away and then at the floor.

"Think about it. What one person in this world would benefit if you were dead?" CJ asked.

"David, my husband," she said slowly, as waves of nausea washed over her and her hands shook again. Someone she once loved and trusted wanted her dead.

"Yes." CJ crossed over to the couch and sat on the edge of it.

"Why didn't you just tell me that to begin with?" Her whole body trembled.

"First, I didn't know if you'd believe me, and second, I didn't want to tell you the other part."

"Well, what is it?" she asked. *How much more is he holding back?*

"They tried to hire me to do it first," CJ said, then looked away.

Anger rushed through her and her face heated. "Oh, really?

Was that before or after we met?" She pushed him away. She couldn't help herself. She had to move. She stood up and started pacing.

CJ blocked her path, his hands parted in front of him, spread like an open book. "Does it matter?" he asked.

"Answer the question." She was tired of all his lies and evasion.

"After, but I turned down the job."

The truth hit her like a bomb. "And that's why they're trying to kill you now, too, because you helped me instead of doing your job?" she whispered.

"Something like that."

"What's going to happen now?"

"Could be they'll stop after this one doesn't call in, but I don't know that for sure," CJ said.

"David's too much. I stopped using his last name; I never liked Watson anyway, but I guess that wasn't enough. David figures if I'm dead, he can have the house and all our assets."

"It's my understanding that it's the life insurance he's mostly after."

"I see."

"The other thing is, I'm not sure I'm the right person to protect you." She watched CJ's face change. He transformed into a very old man in front of her eyes.

"Why not?"

"You'd be dead now if you hadn't stepped up to defend yourself tonight. I screwed up. I dropped my gun when the man bumped into me. But the truth is I shouldn't have used you as bait to begin with. It's not the first time I've fucked up either, and put a loved one in danger." He sunk into the chair and covered his eyes.

Rylee stood over him. "Oh, so you're not superhuman, and I've moved into the 'loved ones' category?"

"This isn't a joke. I'm washed up, losing my game. I got into this racket in the first place because I couldn't protect someone I loved.

I don't want to leave the business the same..." CJ covered his whole face with his hands.

She crawled onto his lap and brushed her hand through his hair. "Tell me about it," she said, gently touching his face.

CJ's shoulders slumped and his mouth opened to say something more, but no words came out at first and he closed it. He lifted his head and looked at her, his voice soft. "Like I told you before, my mum was beaten and died, but there was more to the story. I was supposed to be home for dinner but instead, I went with friends and then stopped at my girlfriend's house. I wasn't there when Mum needed me most, and tonight I wasn't there either—"

"You couldn't know your mother would be attacked. A young person needs to go with his friends." She ran her fingers along his cheek and wiped a tear out his eye. "It's so long ago. It's alright to grieve. You lost somebody you loved but you're not responsible."

"Babies cry. Men do something about it," CJ said, his body suddenly straightening and one hand clenching.

"Who told you that?" she asked.

"My dad." CJ lowered his head.

"You can't control everything, even if you want to." She kissed his cheek. "There's no one else I want with me when the shit hits the fan than you." CJ raised his head and looked into her eyes. "Each person in this life is responsible for themselves, and if you hadn't given me the knife, I couldn't have done anything. You've already helped me in more ways than you'll ever know," Rylee said, and kissed his forehead.

# Chapter 11
# Remember Like I'm Telling You

"How do you get over killing someone?" Rylee asked, sitting on CJ's lap, playing with the collar of his shirt. She wanted to know because right now she felt nothing, but maybe later....

"You didn't have a choice," CJ said.

"I lost it. I don't know what happened, ahh...."

"I did it. I picked up the knife and I stabbed him," CJ said.

"But you didn't, that's not what happened, I—"

"No," he interrupted. "You did nothing. All that time laying in the bed waiting must have gotten to you. He wanted to kill you. Remember, you were frightened."

"But—"

"It's over. Remember it the way I'm telling you. It's easier this way." CJ's eyes were closed, his lips pressed tight. "If you're sticking with me, we need a plan." He opened his eyes.

She gazed into his gray eyes, the color of foggy winter days. "I have a plan."

He tilted his head to one side. "What's that?" His body posture perked up.

Rylee pressed her chest into his. "To share your bed." She felt CJ's suddenly hard dick pressing against her rear. "Is that a yes?" She laughed and glanced at her lap.

"Definitely." A genuine smile spread across his face. "Come then," he continued, taking her wrist, helping her off his lap, and leading her into the bedroom. Thankfully he'd cleaned it, and nothing remained from what had happened earlier. "Let me look at you," he said, unbuttoning the man's shirt she was wearing.

"Umm...I don't know." *Shit, he's undressing me, and I don't want him to see...*

"What don't you know?" He gazed at her with sudden focus, and she didn't want that.

"Could you dim the lights a little?" she asked.

His expression changed to surprise, "But I want to feast my eyes on you," he said lustily, reaching the last button and holding both sides of the shirt, ready to swing them open.

"Wait!" she called out, holding onto the edges of her shirt. "I need to warn you...umm...I lost some...my body...I have—"

"What are you trying to say?" CJ's voice had grown gentle.

"I'm a little wrinkly," she said, crossing her arms in front of her and staring at the floor.

CJ touched her shoulder. "Don't worry about your wrinkles. I've got them too."

"Not like mine." She shook her head no for emphasis and held onto her shirt, keeping it closed.

"Can we worry about our wrinkles later and enjoy ourselves now?" CJ asked. He let go of her shirt. "Take the shirt off," he said firmly, his eyes not leaving her.

"Hmm. I don't know if..." She took a step backward and gave a slow nod but didn't know what to say. Rylee wanted to feel good about her body and knew CJ was right. They should enjoy them-selves. She bowed, exhaled, slid one sleeve off then the other, and let the garment slide to the floor.

"Yer beautiful, like I pictured you," CJ breathed. He led her to his bed. "Lay down, my queen." He pulled the sheet back and arranged the quilt so she could climb in. As she looked up from the mattress, he removed his shirt, then his ribbed sleeveless under-shirt and his slacks, and stood in front of her with a wicked smile. He held on to his jockeys, slid them to the floor, and spun around to show her his backside. He was the beautiful one. He had sharply defined muscles, with tribal black tattoos on his thighs and buttocks. When he faced her again, Rylee's eyes traveled to his cock. A smile spread across her face. She hadn't expected that.

"What do you think?" CJ asked as she stared at his cock.

"I love it. I knew you were uncircumcised, but I don't remember feeling...you having these on the plane," she laughed lightly.

"I don't wear my jewelry all the time; especially when travel-ing...metal body piercings can set off alarms from metal detectors at the airport."

"Will I feel it?" His penis was pierced with gold bars; one through his foreskin and two more in various areas of his cock.

"You'll feel it all. I'll make sure of it." He climbed beside her, placed his hand on her breasts, massaging them, and brought his tongue to her nipples, swirling around them, nibbling and sucking. Her pussy moistened and clenched with need.

"And you wanted to turn the lights off, you shy one." He smiled and brought his fingers to her pussy. He stroked her pubic area, his fingers teasing her. He crawled down and brought his tongue to her clit, licking and sucking. She tried to move away, but he got an arm on top of her stomach and held it there. Rylee couldn't move and was close to coming when he moved one hand to her breast, found her nipple, and squeezed it. "Oh my God," she panted as he continued to pleasure and torture her, bringing his tongue inside her, fucking her with it, and then back to her clit, again and again, licking and biting.

She exploded. Her body shook, and waves of pleasure flooded through her. She cried out, "CJaaaaay!"

"There you go, love," he said, bringing his face up to her. Lit by the lamp on the table, he licked his lips. "You're a good one, a vintage year for sure. Help me with this," he said, handing her a small foil package.

"What is it?" she asked.

"Must have been awhile," he laughed while winking. "It's a condom. Surely you've seen one before."

"I'm sorry. David had a vasectomy." She held it in her hands, unmoving. "I don't know what to do."

CJ laughed. "I'll show you." He took it back, tearing off the wrapper and placing the opening of the condom over his pierced cock. "Now, you can help me bring it up. Take one side."

"Won't your jewelry tear it? Do you really need to wear this? I've only been with one man," she said, pulling it over his cock.

"How many women has your man been with? Do you know for sure?"

"You have a point...but truthfully, I haven't slept with him for over a year, maybe longer."

"I wear a condom, so you don't need to worry about who I've been with. Once we've been together awhile, we can sort this out and go bareback. Come to the edge of the bed, stay on your back and open your legs. I'd like to take you while I stand. The bed's high enough. I want to watch your face."

His saying that made her blush. She tried what he said but her rear hung off, and she hoped she didn't fall off the bed. CJ bent over, grabbed the side of each hip, lifted her to bring her pussy up to the head of his cock, and pushed in slowly. Then he brought it out. CJ's cock was more prominent than David, but because she was wet from already coming, he was able to use her juices to ease entry and pushed in further and further until he was all the way inside of her.

"You feel grand, so tight," he said. He pulled himself out again, but this time he thrust back in hard and fast, making her gasp. He stared down at her face, his eyes never leaving her. "Wrap your legs around me, luv. Hold me tight." He continued to thrust into her, grunting. Sweat formed on his forehead and chest as she held onto his shoulders, and with one final thrust, a firebomb seemed to explode inside of her. He convulsed as his hands held onto her hips, and his eyes softened. When he was done, he caressed her head and looked into her eyes. "I'm sorry I didn't last longer, but you excite me. I promise, next time I will."

A few minutes later when she glanced over, CJ was asleep, but she couldn't get in that state herself. At first, she replayed him sucking on her clit and fucking her, but the prior event kept creeping in. Rylee wanted to remember it like Connor had instructed but couldn't. She recalled the waiting, her fear, bringing the knife down, cutting through her attacker's flesh repeatedly, and the life draining out of the man's face when Connor turned the light on. But what kept her awake was the disturbing thought, *I killed a man and don't feel remorse. I'm numb. What's wrong with me?*

# Chapter 12
# Mazzie Rutherford and Letters of Resignation

"The bee represents hard work, diligence
and orderliness."

— —Unknown

C onnor woke up early and saw that Rylee was still asleep. She looked magnificent. The sheet was thrown over the bottom part of her leg, but the rest of her lay in his bed exposed. He could get lost in her flesh forever. He traced freckles on her shoulder and lay a hand on her breast, caressing it. The room was still cool and shadowy, her creamy white flesh surrounded by the dark purple hues in the room reminding him of a Renaissance painting.

It was clear to Connor that the agency wasn't going to stop without him going on the offensive, even though he told Rylee something different because he didn't want her worrying. He needed to send the agency a message, but couldn't take her with him or leave her alone here—too dangerous.

She could probably stay with Maggie, his neighbor. If anyone dared show up at her place, the booby-trap bombs she had planted all around the outside of her home would blow them to kingdom come. If they somehow got in the house, her Doberman/Pit bull crew of three would tear them apart; that's if Maggie herself didn't shoot their balls off. There were times even Connor was afraid of her. Rylee would be safe with her.

Connor closed his eyes and pressed his cock against Rylee's backside. *Someday soon*, he thought. His hands trembled as he touched her hips and thought of ways to make it enjoyable for her. He closed his eyes, imagining it, making a mental list of what he would need and how to proceed. Massage oil, smaller dildo and—

"You're awake already?" Rylee asked, reaching for the sheet, covering herself, and ending Connor's fantasy.

* * *

Connor wasn't sure Maggie liked her, but she didn't like anyone. She even had harsh words for Connor. You should have called me before popping in," she said, the dogs barking and growling in the background. She glared at the laundry room where she'd locked them and moved closer to him.

Maggie's place was nothing like his. Her house was a bunker decorated by a hoarder. There were pathways inside the house for walking, but her various items filled the walls and pushed out into the room. Old newspapers, car parts, boxes of metal pieces, knives, and old kitchen supplies spilled everywhere. The stairs leading to the second level even had possessions piled on them. Perhaps Rylee will like the books that lined the stairway.

"She can't stay. I don't have room," Maggie said, her voice firm and her jaw tense as she shuttled the dogs out the kitchen door.

"There's men trying to kill her," Connor said. "I have a job in

Dublin. We had to kill a man last night who'd come for her. She can't stay at my cottage."

"What did she do?" Maggie's eyebrows shot up, her eyes wide as she looked over at Rylee, her mouth curled in a gleeful smile.

"Left her husband."

"Is that all? Pffff." Maggie waved her hands back and forth. "Two of mine tried that. One's in the ground on the property, but I don't have to tell you, do I, Connie?"

"How about the attic?" Connor asked.

"No, none of my exes in the attic." Maggie looked around, pretending someone might be listening.

"Please, Maggie, this isn't a joke. We need your help."

"Alright, Connie, for you." She patted his hand. "Don't worry about a thing. She can use the attic room and I'll keep her safe. If I have any trouble, I'll call for backup. Patrick Kelly and his crew live close by." Maggie looked over at Rylee and explained, "The second floor has a secret staircase and no one knows about it but Connie here."

"I brought the cat, too, and her litterbox. I'll bring it in," Connor said.

"Not the damn cat. What about my dogs?"

"Clover can stay with Rylee in the attic," Connor said. "She needs some clothes, too. Can she borrow some things?"

"Should I roll out a red carpet too?" Maggie asked, staring at him. She turned to Rylee. "Hopefully you like camo pants, wife beaters and sweats." She then stomped towards the kitchen.

"Anything clean would be fine," Rylee called after her, her arms crossed in front, protecting herself as if Maggie meant to do bodily harm.

"Do you cook?" Maggie asked, turning back to Rylee.

"I love to cook."

"Wonderful. I hate to cook, so you can make dinners. Check out the pantry and freezer. I like to eat at five." Maggie left the room and slipped out the kitchen door. Connor went to the car and got the cat's things as Rylee inspected the kitchen.

* * *

You okay with the room, then?" Connor asked as they stood outside and he prepared to leave. He noticed Rylee's nervousness. She scratched her arms and ran her hands through her hair.

"Yes, it's comfy with a birds-eye of everything," she said, biting her bottom lip.

"Maggie's good people. Give her a chance. You'll warm to her."

"If I can warm to a hitman, I'm sure I'll warm to her, whatever she is..."

Connie brought her closer, their bodies pressed together. She touched the buttons on his shirt and nuzzled his neck when he leaned down. "I should tell you, Maggie and—" He suddenly stopped talking and looked out in the distance.

"Tell me what?"

"We'll talk about it later," Connor said. She folded her arms around herself and walked with him to the Tesla. Connor reached for her hand. It was clammy, and her fingers trembled. "What's wrong?'

"I'm nervous about staying here without you," she said, her eyes blinking rapidly. "What if—"

"Always keep the stairs pulled up. If anyone shows up, Maggie will keep them busy, and she'd never tell them about you. They'll never find the panel or those stairs. You'll be safe."

"I wish you didn't have to leave," she whispered in his ear. "What are you going to do?"

"Send a message."

"Be careful."

"I will, more so now that I have you."

She buried her head in his chest. The closeness they shared

last night was still there. It pained him to leave Rylee, but he had to. He turned away and climbed into the car.

* * *

"Did Connie tell you we dated?" Maggie asked later, leaning against the refrigerator, crossing her hands across her chest and squinting.

"What?"

"Ha, I didn't think so," Maggie smirked. "He's cagey. The truth is that we were engaged once, but we're too much alike." She paused. "Nothing to say?"

"What *can* I say?"

"Don't worry, I'm not going to hurt you or anything." She reached by the side of the refrigerator and picked up her rifle. "I'm over Connie, and truthfully, he's had too many women for me to get jealous anymore, but I can honestly say you don't seem his type at all."

"What's his type?"

"Extremes. Athletes or glamour girls. You don't seem to check either box. What do you do, besides stirring your husband up enough to put a hit out on you?"

"Write books."

"What kind?"

"Ahh, contemporary romance suspense."

"Living one of your stories, are ya? I don't think this is going to end with any happily-ever-after with Connie. He's not the settling-down type. Never even got close after me," Maggie said.

"Scared him away from women, did you?" Rylee asked, hoping to make Maggie leave her alone.

"A live one. Good to know."

Rylee stared her down, holding a book as a shield. "I don't need his dating history, and if I do, I'll ask him about it."

"Fine. I have work to do." Maggie stomped out the kitchen door with her rifle under her arm.

* * *

Rylee stopped on the steps and selected a few more books to take to her room. She lifted the attic steps and put the panel in place. Some loud meows and scratching came from the front of the carrier. She let Clover out, and the cat settled in her lap. *Why didn't he tell me about Maggie?* Men were all alike—dishonest. She was getting too involved too fast anyway. This was the wake-up call she needed. Maggie called it; *I'm not his type.* She ran her hand through Clover's fur as she purred. Having the cat on her lap was a comfort while she accepted that her relationship with CJ couldn't go anywhere.

She spent the rest of the evening stacking boxes against the eave to give her more room in the attic. When she cleaned under the bed, one small box she found tipped over as she piled it with the rest of them, spilling pictures and bundled-up letters on the floor. There were photographs of Maggie and CJ together.

Maggie hadn't lied. They were once a couple. There was a small stack of letters held with a red ribbon. Rylee sat down and pulled on either end of the bow, and the papers came loose on her lap. She read them all and after she was done, she realized CJ had once loved Maggie. But it didn't matter; he left her anyway. *He's not the kind of man that will stay, and he likely still has unresolved feelings for Maggie. I need to let him go before he hurts me.*

She gathered all the contents, returned them to the box and slammed the lid. Dust floated in the air and caught in the remaining sunlight like gold glitter. She put the box with all the others. Rylee made the bed with washed linens, covered them with a plaid wool blanket, and placed a slim pillow at the top, flattened by all the heads that had lain on it night after night. Maybe CJ had laid his head there, too. She smoothed the pillowcase and punched it down, leaving an indentation where his head should be in the middle of the pillow.

Rylee thumbed through the books she'd brought upstairs, deciding which one to read, and settled on the one by Mazzie Rutherford. She turned it over to read the blurb and her eyes landed on the author's headshot. OMG! She recognized the woman—the same one with the walker from the locker room at the Gaylord who told her she needed to have more confidence in herself. She had met Mazzie Rutherford, one of this century's most successful romance authors. Rylee chuckled. "Wait until I tell Sheila," she wistfully said out loud to herself.

Monday

Connor needed to send a message. This time he'd be the one to attack. With Rylee safely ensconced at Maggie's, he drove to Dublin, checked into a hotel, and got a good's night sleep.

He had never met his handler, Archie, in person, but two years ago the guy had slipped up, sending something by email using his real IP address. Connor had taken the opportunity to send it to his friend, a computer whiz, who'd come up with a location and background check. The report said the man was an ex-pat American living in Dublin, a Yale graduate, and known as a troll on several social media sites. It sounded right. Connor would confirm if his handler was the same man as soon as he heard the voice.

Connor watched Archie's apartment, a brick rowhome in Merrion Square, one of the better sections. The man leaving looked the right age, thirty-five or so. Red-haired, a bit overweight. After the man left, Connor approached the building. He put on his gloves and gained entry when another occupant left and held the door for him. He examined the mailboxes in the vestibule. Apartment 101 read "A. Harold." There was only one apartment on the first floor.

Connor knocked, just in case Archie didn't live alone. No one answered. In less than a minute, he was inside. He walked around the apartment, looking for cameras or devices that might relay his presence to the man. There was nothing. He searched Archie's desk, but it held nothing but a calendar and a computer. When Connor touched the keyboard, the screen bounced to life. It wasn't password-protected, making him think he maybe had the wrong guy. Anyone who worked for the agency would never.... But one email window was still open, and Connor recognized the name of the sender, David Watson. His eyes widened as he read it:

*You have until Wednesday midnight to finish the job. I will find someone else if it's not completed by that time. I'm tired of the incompetence of your people.*

Connor attempted opening other saved items on the computer, but they were locked files. There were thousands of them. Archie's laptop was a goldmine of information if he could read any of it. He searched the apartment, found a bag in the closet, brought it back, unplugged the laptop, and shoved it in the tote. He was sure his computer expert friend, if given the time, could unlock these files; and if he did, Connor would be able to use the information against the agency if forced to. Extra insurance to keep Rylee and him alive.

Connor moved forward with his plan to handle Archie. Simple is best, according to Pally, so he waited next to Archie's front door. This would have been a suitable plan if Archie had returned in a reasonable amount of time, a half-hour or even an hour. However, three hours later, Archie still had not returned and Connor had lost his ability to be attentive. He took a break, removed a bottle of water from the refrigerator, pulled a chair from the desk, sat by the window, and looked for his mark, becoming angry. An hour later, his handler, juggling two bags of groceries and a four-pack of Guinness, walked towards his domicile. Connor got up from the chair and returned it to the desk. He poured the rest of the water on the carpet in the middle of the floor, threw the bottle there, unzipped his pants, and pissed on top of it. By this time, he had to go, and there was no time to use the facilities and get behind the front door. He knew finding DNA in urine was difficult and only lasted a short time. He also knew the police would not become involved at all if the agency was the first to discover the scene.

Connor picked the gun off the windowsill and approached the front door, standing to the side of it, well out of his victim's line of vision, and waited. He heard the slamming of the vestibule door. Seconds later, the doorknob turned, and his handler entered, not noticing him. "What the fuck is this?" man asked indignantly when seeing the wet stain on his rug.

Connor recognized the voice. "Did you send anyone else?" he asked from beside the door, startling the man.

Archie turned and cried, "No!" and ran towards him. *POW KPOW*. Archie's head bounced backward, the Tesco grocery bags flying from his hands, the contents spilling out, his body hitting the floor with a thud. Oranges and apples rolled from the bag, across the living room floor and under the desk. A box of Lucky Charms landed upside down, and a leprechaun stood on his head and frowned at him.

Connor kicked the apartment door closed and let the scene settle around him. He picked up the pen and wrote on a piece of paper:

*Consider this my letter of resignation.*

*Sincerely,*

*CJ*

.  .  .

He placed the letter on top of Archie's body, along with the wallet from the assassin Rylee cut down. When Archie didn't check in with the agency, they'd send someone to investigate why, and when they did...

Connor smiled, placed the pen in his pocket, picked up an apple, stuck it in his other pocket, hoisted the computer bag over his shoulder, and slipped out the door with his gloves still on.

# Chapter 13
# Climb Aboard

 Tuesday morning

It was early or late, depending on how you look at things. Connor was taking a chance by arriving at Maggie's at this time in the morning. He'd made a stop already, hiding the laptop, where it would never be found until he could make other arrangements. He parked the car and made a lot of noise, slamming the car door and coughing several times. He would've called her if she had a cellphone, but she didn't believe in them. Hopefully, Maggie wouldn't be startled and accidentally blow him away.

"Stop right there," Maggie's voice rang out.

"It's me, Connor."

"Got done early. Didn't expect you until much later."

"I stopped in to check on things before I knock off the other one."

"Yer going to kill her husband, then?"

"I'm leaning that way."

"If you do that, she'll know it was you. Do you really think she can live with that?"

"He's hired an assassin to kill her and hasn't given up."

"That may be, but if you love her, my advice is not to do it. She'll always be looking at you sideways."

"What else can I do?"

"Find a different way to get the same result," Maggie said. "Then you really love her, eh?"

"Yes, I really do."

"Are ya going to wake her? You won't get up there without knocking and getting her to drop the steps."

"No. I'll sleep in the car."

"There's always my bed, for old times' sake," Maggie chuckled.

"What did you tell her?" An overwhelming sense of dread spread through him.

"The truth, something you neglected."

"Are you trying to blow me out of the water?" How could he fix this?

"Of course not. I'm trying to see how serious the both of you are. Goodnight or Good morning. I'm going to bed." Maggie turned and entered the house, leaving Connor surrounded in darkness.

Rylee dropped the stairs down, but before she could take a step, Connor climbed up. "I'm back," he said, reaching the top and walking towards her.

Anger she didn't know she had rushed through her. "When were you going to tell me you were engaged to Maggie?" She wanted to say more but struggled to speak.

Connor backed up in surprise. "I was going to, but—"

"Stop it," she screamed. "I'm not getting involved with another cheater. If you want Maggie, go to her. Don't use me as an excuse to come back to her."

"What are you talking about?"

Hiding me here, in your ex's house? A convenient ploy."

"That's enough," Connor said. "You're not the person I thought you were if you think that." He headed for the stairs, placing one foot on the step and then another until he disappeared and passed into the hallway below.

Rylee sat down on the bed in misery, her hands covering her face. *Why did I act so irrational and desperate?* Clover came out from under the bed and wrapped around Rylee's feet, purring, its gold eyes peering up at her. She reached down and pet it and the cat arched its back, wanting more. She got up from the bed and ran to the window after she heard the sound of tires crunching on gravel. Connor was driving away. She gulped back tears, and her stomach heaved. *What have I done?*

* * *

*Damn Maggie, why couldn't she keep her mouth shut?* Connor's hands gripped the steering wheel, and he tried to force everything out of his mind but couldn't, his jaw tightening. Maggie could never leave well enough alone. Always looking for trouble. He was surprised about Rylee. He hadn't seen her as the jealous type before. He slapped the steering wheel with his hand. What the fuck should he do about her husband? He had been planning to discuss it with Rylee and get her okay. He suspected the agency would back down after they found Archie's body, the wallet of the other dead operative, and the computer gone. His eyes blinked, and he nervously pulled on his ear, thinking about his next move. He needed to discuss it with someone. He would arrive at

Shannon Airport in five minutes. He'd have time to call before the plane boarded.

After Connor parked, he opened the Kakoa app. He sent a text from his burner to Domenic:

> R u available4chat?
>
> I did it. Took kitty and quit
>
> Shit hit fan. 3 of theirs down
>
> Thinking about husband, he started it
>
> Opinion?

Nothing. Was Domenic just not available? He hoped it wasn't anything else. He pushed the phone back into his pocket, grabbed his bag, and waited for the shuttle.

The plane landed in Philadelphia on time, at three pm. Connor had no problem picking up his rental and finding David's house in Greenville, Delaware. He remembered the street address from Rylee's license. He cruised by the house in a neighborhood with other spacious homes on large lots. He spotted no cars in the driveway, although there could be someone home and they simply parked in the garage.

Connor found a park nearby, right behind the house, and left his car in the parking lot there. A walking path went right behind the houses—convenient. He went deeper into the woods and watched the back and sides of the house for activity. There was no activity for twenty minutes, but just as Connor was considering moving closer to the home and investigating, a luxury sports car pulled up. An older man and a younger woman spilled out, leaning into one another, stumbling up to the front door. The man was shorter than he imagined. His dyed hair and bottled skin appeared almost orange. Connor didn't anticipate him putting up too much of a fight.

The woman dressed differently than Rylee, but Connor didn't find it sexy. Her blouse was cut too low, and her skirt was short and tight. She wore stilettos at least four inches high, towering over Rylee's husband and looking tougher than him. He would rather not deal with the woman; but shaking his head, he realized he might not have a choice. Maybe he could find a way to make her leave. If she did, he wouldn't have to kill her too. His stomach churned.

* * *

"What's on the menu?" Maggie asked, coming in the back door and tracking dirt all over the floor with her dogs in tow.

"Carrot soup," Rylee replied, pouring the steaming orange liquid into their bowls and placing a basket of garlic bread on the table.

"That's all?" Maggie asked, eyes scanning the table before sitting down. "Do I look like a rabbit? I'm a grown woman. I need more to eat than this after working all day."

"I made a salad, too, and there's the garlic bread." She spread her hands like a magician.

"I guess that'll have to do," Maggie said, dipping her spoon into the bowl, blowing on it and then sipping from it. "It's too spicy. What's in it?" She spit some back in the bowl, then picked up her water and gulped it down, her face flushed.

"Just carrots, celery, water, oat milk and ginger," Rylee said, taking a spoonful herself.

"Too much ginger," Maggie said.

"Ginger's good for the digestive system."

"Not if you don't like it." Maggie bit into a piece of garlic bread and pushed the soup bowl away. "What is it with you and food? Why does everything you eat have to *do* something? Food should be enjoyable. If it isn't, why even bother?" She finished eating the bread.

"I don't understand why food can't be both healthy and enjoyable."

"Well, you haven't proved it to me."

"I'll keep working on it."

"Please don't. I heard you and Connor having a row this morning?"

"I wouldn't say that, exactly."

"What would you call it?"

"A discussion where we figured things out," Rylee answered confidently.

"And what did you figure out, dear?"

"He's not ready for a relationship."

"*Pffft*. Don't be a gowl. He drove all the way back here before leaving for Philadelphia, when he could have easily flown from Dublin. He told me himself he's serious. Even chewed me out for telling you we dated before he could tell you. Most likely, *you're* the one not ready." Maggie picked up a fork full of salad and stuffed it in her mouth.

"Well, I, I, I'm—"

"You either are or you aren't. Which one is it?" Maggie asked. "I don't want you messing with Connie's head if you aren't serious. He's putting himself on the line for you. Can't think of many men willing ta lay everything on the line for a woman." Maggie glared and took another bite of salad.

"Wait a minute. Why's he going to Philadelphia?"

"I'm sure you can figure that out." Maggie lowered her fork to her plate. "I thought you said you're a writer." She picked up her bowl and salad plate, pursed her lips, rolled her eyes, walked to the sink, dumped the soup down the drain, and walked out the door.

* * *

After she cleaned the kitchen and loaded the dishwasher, Rylee stepped out on the porch. She watched Maggie herd the sheep towards the barn as the sun disappeared behind the hills, streaks of purple and orange filling the sky. Her hands rested on the grey wicker arms of the chair, patinaed by weather and time. *Is Connor going to Philadelphia to kill David?*She hated David, but most women going through a divorce probably hated their husbands. She didn't actually want him dead. Or did she? He had hired someone to kill *her*, after all. He deserved to die. But Rylee didn't let her mind travel there. She just wanted David to split the assets of their marriage and then leave her alone. She'd already killed one man and didn't want to be responsible for another. Besides, when ex-husbands turn up dead, the police always suspect the ex-wife. Maggie had said Connor was serious about her, and she'd driven him away with jealousy. Maybe she had inadvertently convinced Connor to kill her husband.

Two black birds suddenly landed on the railing, like some kind of omen. *Caw! Caw!* one bird called to the other, stretching out and flapping its wings. *BLAM!* A gunshot rang out. One bird flew away while the other was blown to bits, blood and feathers exploding everywhere. With feathers and bird blood pasted on her face and clothing, Rylee ducked, scurrying down from the porch. The dogs locked in the house were barking frantically. She peeked over the railing and saw Maggie running towards the barn, and heard more shots being fired, this time towards the other woman. Where were they coming from?

Rylee scanned the front of the barn and the fields on either side. In the late sunset, she could barely make out a black knit hat popping up, worn by a man crouched by the fence near the hay pile. His other clothing was black too. His arm was bent and his hand gripped a rifle, ready to fire again. Suddenly another shot rang out, and his head jerked back. He rolled on the ground and his rifle fell out of his hands.

Rylee left the porch and walked closer. Maggie came out of the barn and stood over him, firing at his body twice and making it twitch. His head rolled to the side, the knit cap partially falling off and blonde hair spilling out. Maggie kicked him, watched for a reaction, then turned, waved to Rylee, and walked towards her. "Don't worry," she called out. "He's no longer a threat. Surprised he knew to come here. I guess he figured Connie and me were neighbors and staked the place out. Saw you outside, most likely. He's a professional, after all, but he didn't do his homework. Should have done more digging on who I was."

"And who are you?" Rylee asked.

"Ex-IRA. Trained by my da and brothers when I was a wee girl. Lost all of them by the time I was sixteen. You should go in the house. I'm going to secure the barn and get rid of the body. If there's one, there could be more." Maggie's eyes traveled the fields.

"I can help you."

"I don't think so. You don't want to get yer hands dirty with this."

"I killed a man at Connor's."

"Sure you did." Maggie laughed and shook her head.

"I did. He attacked me in bed, when Connor couldn't get to him in time. I snapped. I stabbed the man. I'm responsible for this one coming too. I need to help."

"I misjudged you," Maggie said, her smile disappearing. She

rubbed the blood off Rylee's cheek using her finger. "I thought you were the delicate type, but here you are, a murderess." Her eyes lit up, a smile returning. "Maybe you're a good match for Connie after all. You can pick up the slack. Let's go." She motioned to the body and then back to Rylee, her orange canvas jacket glinting against the darkening indigo sky.

# Chapter 14
# The Diary

Tuesday evening

Connor waited until dark before touring the outside of Rylee's soon-to-be dead ex-husband's house. As he reached the back, he heard a door slam and pressed himself against the side of the building, creeping forward until he could see the long stone driveway where the car was parked. He smiled with delight at the woman he saw walk in with David now leaving alone, wearing a red sequined dress. She climbed into the driver's seat, started the engine, and backed down the drive. David was now alone. Perfect.

Connor glanced up at the home. Most of the lights that were on were up on the upper level. Most likely his target was up there. He jimmied the sliding door and entered a large family room connected to an open kitchen area. He removed his gun and heard a television coming from somewhere as he found the steps to the upper floor. He followed the sound of the television and arrived in the master bedroom, a gigantic plasma screen hanging on the wall, blaring FOX News. He heard water running from the bathroom and singing. Killing him in the shower would keep the mess contained and wash away DNA, but Connor still wasn't sure he was going to kill him. It might drive Rylee away, if she wasn't gone already. Connor's other option was to put the fear of God into David and encourage him to do the right thing, give Rylee a fair and equitable divorce and stay away from her. If he did that, Connor would let him live; and if he didn't, he'd come back and terminate him. If David had half a brain, he'd choose life.

Connor sat down in the burgundy leather wing chair in the corner of the bedroom and waited, watching the TV report that crime was down a second year in a row in Wilmington. Hopefully it would stay that way. The shower went on forever, making him think that David was more like a teenaged girl. It struck him that the room was decorated in a very masculine style—the leather chair, the colors, the dark walls. None of it looked like Rylee Reed.

The water stopped running abruptly, then Connor heard the slapping of feet on tile, a towel rubbing skin, and whistling. Seconds later, David entered the room with his head down, a towel wrapped around his waist, carrying a glass of something amber. He didn't notice Connor. He whistled some more as a crime show played in the background. He stopped and tilted his head back, chugging the rest of the drink, and when he was done he finally saw Connor. He froze, his mouth falling open and his eyes widening. "Who are..." he began, but then his words dried up in mid-sentence. "What do you want?"

Then he threw the glass at Connor's head, hitting him. It cut his skin and blood started to flow as David ran for the door. Connor's anger exploded as he jumped on the man. All he wanted to do now was kill him, as violently and painfully as possible. Somehow, though, he pulled himself together. "That was a mistake," he said, drops of blood dropping onto David's face as he straddled him, sticking the barrel of the gun in his mouth.

"Is this about my wife?" David mumbled, barely able to talk.

"Good guess," Conner replied. "I'll make this simple to keep you from wetting yourself. You have one chance and one chance only to turn this around and save your life. If you don't take the gift I'm giving you, there'll be no second chances. Give your wife half of everything and then stay out of her life. No more assassination attempts. Got it?" Connor pulled the gun away from the man's teeth.

David took in a slow breath and closed his eyes. "Yes, I agree."

"Don't make me come back."

"Is Rylee coming back?"

"No, she's under my protection now, so shove any ideas of sending anyone after her. I've already killed three of your men. Next time I come for you. Understand?"

"Yes."

"Is there anyone else still running around out there?"

Connor watched the man's eyes grow large, then look to the side. He quietly said, "Yes."

"Who?" Connor asked, bringing the gun back to the man's mouth.

"I don't know. It's just a phone number."

"Where did you get it?"

"One of my clients who's serving time."

"Get up. Call him. Tell him the job's cancelled."

Connor watched as David climbed off the floor and picked his phone up from the nightstand. He turned it on and scrolled through recent calls, until landing on one number and hitting redial. "Yes, I want the job cancelled. I've changed my mind." He hung up and turned to Connor. "Voice mail."

"You better hope he gets it in time, or I'll have to cancel him myself, and then you too." Connor got up and moved towards the door.

"Where should I send the settlement documents and funds?" David asked.

"We'll send an address."

Connor backed out of the room, walked down the hall, and left the house. As he drove to the airport, he reflected on how amazing it was he was able to keep his cool even after someone had physically hurt him. He realized he had done it for Rylee.

\* \* \*

He had an open return, but unfortunately Connor couldn't book anything out until Wednesday afternoon. He stayed at a hotel near the airport. If the other people contracted to do David's job couldn't pull their man... He subdued his anxiety with some deep breathing. Rylee wasn't at the cottage, so even if the assassin did show, he wouldn't be able to find her.

Before the plane departed the next day, he tried Domenic again on his burner. There was still no answer to his text so he sent another, and another after that. Nothing. Connor knew something was wrong. In all the time he had known Domenic, he had always responded, even if it sometimes took him a few hours. Did the agency somehow track him down? A wave of nausea caused him to make a break for the lavatory, but a flight attendant called out, "Sir, please take a seat, we're taking off shortly." Connor ignored him, yanking the door open and heaving into the toilet before returning to his seat.

Another half hour and they were still sitting on the runway. The pilot announced, "Ladies and gentleman, we apologize for the delay, but unfortunately we will need to disembark. Another plane will be readied. Please return to the boarding area and wait for future announcements concerning your flight. Please don't forget to take your personal belongings with you." *Shit,* Connor thought to himself.

\* \* \*

Rylee sat on her bed, looking out the window and scanning the horizon for cars. He should be back by now. Did something happen to him? She pet Clover as she curled up on her lap, purring and kneading her thighs with her claws. She sighed. It seemed like it had been months ago that she'd attended the conference at the Gaylord, but today would only make it one week. So much had happened. She'd discovered her husband was worse than she thought possible, while a man who killed for a living could save her life. She reached for her notebook and, as she did, Clover jumped off her lap to the window ledge and settled in again, warming herself in the early morning sun. She began writing, "I never thought I'd die like this, in the Atlantic Ocean..."

Thursday morning

Rylee needed to swim. The water would cleanse her of everything that she had done, including stabbing a man and assisting Maggie in disposing of a body by feeding it to pigs. All she had to swim in was borrowed underwear, so she put Connor's shirt and a pair of Maggie's sweats over them and started walking.

It took her over an hour to reach the water; it looked close by, but it was an optical illusion. The gray ocean reminded her of Connor's eyes. She scanned the ocean, her thoughts rolling with the movement of the water and then becoming lost in the waves. The water was rougher here, almost like when she had visited Baja, Mexico so long ago. She needed to be careful and not go out too far.

She slipped off her borrowed shoes and tossed her shirt on the sand. She bent down and examined her red toe, just a blister, caused by the looseness of Maggie's shoes. She dipped her toe in the water and pulled it out again. It was too cold, but it numbed the pain from her blister.

There was no easy way to go in, so she just ran towards the water, screaming, stepping on stones and shells. If she stopped, she'd chicken out. She reached a point where the ground under her dropped away, the sand collapsed, and her body became immersed. The more she swam, the warmer her body became. She looked back at the beach and noticed her white shirt farther to the right than when she'd first entered. She swam towards it, but no matter what she did, the ocean kept pulling her left. She drifted further and further out and away from shore.

She scanned the beach, searching for help. Suddenly she saw a dark figure walking down the beach and she waved at them, hoping to get their attention. She wasn't sure if they saw her or not. They seemed to watch, then turned their back and proceeded in the opposite direction. She screamed out in anger, "No, no, no!" and slapped the waves with her arm. Eventually, the figure transformed into a dot. Tired, she flipped on her back and floated, staring at the cloudy sky. *Is this how I'm going to die?*

\* \* \*

Connor arrived at Maggie's late on Thursday morning. It was eerily quiet. Where were the dogs? They always barked when someone came. He drew his gun and proceeded to the door. He didn't knock but simply tried the door, which turned out to be unlocked. Maggie would never make that kind of mistake. Instead of entering, he walked the perimeter, looking in the windows, but saw no one. His head buzzed with anxiety.

He headed to the barn and found her, dead and laying on a pile of hay, a bullet hole in the back of her head. Someone had surprised her. Where was Rylee? He stared at Maggie's body in disbelief. *Impossible.* How had they gotten the drop on her? He scrambled to understand what had happened. His chest tingled and his stomach clenched. He listened and heard scratching, approaching the noise coming from the tack room. As he clutched his gun, he opened the door and stepped aside. The dogs hurled towards him, the Doberman taking him off his feet, then bounding towards Maggie's body, stopping, sniffing his mistress and licking her face. The pit bulls followed. Soon after that, the howling started. Connor cried with the dogs and tried to calm them, but they were inconsolable.

Finally he grabbed hold of the Doberman, Buster, and led him back to the tack room, the other dogs following. He closed the door, wiped the tears from his eyes, and tried to pull himself together. Whoever had shot Maggie could've taken Rylee, but why would they when they were supposed to kill her? Maybe her body was somewhere else on the property. He walked to the back of the barn and searched the grounds until he reached the pig pen. The pigs were all in the middle, eating, and as Connor watched he realized what they were gnawing at. He backed away, then made himself go back. As he got closer, he realized that what remained of the corpse was clearly male. Maybe the assassin killed Maggie after he discovered the other man's body. He must have surprised her when she had come to let the sheep out, not giving her a chance to do the same thing to him.

Connor continued to search for Rylee, walking back towards Maggie's house. He entered the home, hoping to find her inside and safely hiding; but when he reached the hall and saw that the attic steps were hanging down, disappointment flooded through him. Connor climbed them, praying he wouldn't find her corpse. Once up in the attic, he saw that Rylee's borrowed things were strewn about, and an open notebook laid on the bed. Connor picked it up and started reading, excitement growing—Rylee's diary. He read what she had written:

*I had to help Maggie last night, but what I saw I can never unsee. I need to cleanse myself. I need to swim in the ocean.*

Connor threw the journal back on the bed and ran to the stairs, climbing down them so fast that he lost his footing and slid to the bottom. From there he ran down the short hallway and out the door. *Did the assassin who killed Maggie see the diary too?*

# Chapter 15
# Revery

"To make a prairie it takes a clover and one
    bee, One clover, and a bee, And
    revery. The revery alone will do, If
    bees are few."

— —Emily Dickinson

Connor jumped in his car, arriving at the beach in less than four minutes. There was another car parked in the lot, a blue sedan. Instead of taking the steps, he crouched down low on the cliff and peeked down. A man was standing, facing the ocean next to a pile of clothing, shoes and glasses. Was he the hitman the other company sent, or just a bystander who stopped to help? Where was Rylee? He scanned the water's horizon line and almost didn't see her, until a hand shot out of a wave and then a head bobbed. He could tell she was struggling, caught in a riptide, trying to swim back in, but the water was pulling her out. But if she did come in, she'd be killed by the man waiting on the beach...if he was the killer.

Anger flooded through Connor. He wanted to go down there, but if the man was armed and a killer, he would need to do it in stealth mode. He pushed his anger down. He had a rifle with a scope in the trunk of the car, but what if the man wasn't a killer? He removed the pistol from his pocket, made sure it was loaded, and made his way down to the beach. He didn't use the designated path but kept low in the grasses and rocks.

He was only ten feet away and still the man stared out at the ocean, unaware that Connor was almost upon him. "You, turn around and put your hands in the air," he shouted, pointing his gun at the man's back.

The man turned around slowly, his hands out in front of him and a funny smile on his face. "You can't save her. I don't have to do anything. The crazy bitch is drowning." Then the man hurled himself at Connor and they wrestled over his gun. Connor held on to it and pushed himself away from the man who was now on the ground below him. He fired, hitting the man in the chest. He fired again and the man didn't move.

He searched the waves for Rylee. He thought he saw something, a horizontal line going in and out of the water. Connor knew he couldn't go in. He'd never learned to swim. Rooted to the spot, his hands clammy, afraid to move, his leg muscles tightened up. He made himself move for Rylee, walking up the beach where he knew the neighbors kept a rowboat for emergencies. It was there with a rope, a life preserver and oars. He shook uncontrollably and licked his lips. "Pull yourself together," he said, but he hesitated. He had to do it. He threw the oars in the boat, dragged it into the water, and pulled it with the rope while still running along the beach, aiming further left from where the riptide seemed to be taking Rylee.

As he watched her, he imagined her screaming for help. His

father screamed too that day, so long ago: "Don't be a coward, Connie! Jump in, for God's sake!" Connor was only six and didn't want to. He wanted nothing to do with swimming. His father, tired of waiting, came out of the pool and threw him in. The water flooded into his nose and down his throat, and he sunk to the bottom and struggled to come to the top. His father was willing to let him drown, but his mum came in and pulled him out. That night, like so many nights before, his mum and father argued. His father's voice rung out, "I'll have no coward for a son." Connor buried his face in the pillow to hide his crying, but he couldn't hide his shame. The following day his father left and never came back.

Connor pushed the memory away. "I'm not a scared lad anymore," he whispered, dragging the boat and aligning it with Rylee's position. He jumped in, picked up the oars and rowed out, searching the water's jagged waves for Rylee. He wouldn't lose someone he loved this time because he was a coward.

*I'm going to die in a different country, alone.* Rylee should have told Maggie where she was going. She'd wasted her life. Instead of doing all the things she had wanted to do, she had done what David wanted her to. Always afraid. On the verge of tears, she stopped herself, laughing to herself, *I'm wet enough already*. Salty water spilled into her mouth. She kept very still, letting the waves move her along. She wasn't going to fight them anymore. She closed her eyes too, to keep the water out as she floated and waves splashed against her.

*Don't be stupid*, she said to herself. She needed to fight for her life like she did when she fought the assassin and killed him. She flipped to her stomach and started paddling again. *I need to see CJ again and tell him I love him.*

She realized right then that every decision you make in life carries a risk, and even with bad ones you learn something. She kept fighting the waves, but more time passed and her arms and legs grew more tired and cold. She turned over again. If she died, she wanted to see the sky.

She opened her eyes, only she didn't see sky. She saw Connor smiling down at her. "Do you want to stay out here or climb aboard?" he asked with a broad smile, reaching out his arms for her.

3 Months Later

As Connor entered their cottage, Maggie's dogs stampeded him. They had adopted them after her death. They needed a home, and neither of them could stand the thought of them ending up euthanized or taken in by bad people. Clover wasn't too happy about it. It had taken them almost an entire day to track her down. She had enjoyed her time on the lam a bit too much after the killer had left the door open.

When the cops found the bodies at Maggie's and then the one at the beach, it brought unwanted heat. Maggie being ex-IRA and then winding up dead brought too much attention from Interpol too. All of those things and the missing computer made the agency back off, and the other company must have wanted no part either. Connor got one simple text: *You win.*

"You've got a piece of mail," Connor announced, pushing the dogs off him. "Picked it up from the post when I dropped the honey order off at McCormick's."

"What is it?" Rylee's eyes were curious as he handed it to her.

"Something from your ex." Rylee held the envelope tentatively. "It's not going to blow up. Open it," Connie said.

She ripped the envelope open slowly and removed some

papers, reading them. "My divorce papers. It's official." She smiled. "I can't believe it."

"Grand, now I can make you my woman."

"I think you already have."

"I mean marry you, lass. What dropped on the floor?" He watched her bend down and retrieve a blue piece of paper. "Your ass looks very lovely and inviting today. Do it again."

"Oh my God, the bastard actually sent me a check," Rylee said, her eyes lighting up as she unfolded the piece of paper, clearly marked out in the amount of $850,000. There was a Post-It note on the back and she read it out loud: "More to follow once the house is out of escrow." She laughed. "I wonder if it'll clear when I deposit it?"

"I've got something to deposit as well," Connor said, squeezing a handful of flesh on her rear. His erection was massive and groaned against the fabric of his pants. He'd fantasized about fucking Rylee the entire drive back. He needed her. He also wanted to tell her about Domenic's call. Turns out he had panicked for nothing. Domenic hadn't responded to Connor's texts because his mother-in-law was sick and he had had to go and take over her care. Connor had it all planned—they would visit Domenic and his wife when they took their honeymoon, and then on the way back stop and see Rylee's best friend, Sheila. He had even bought a ring.

Connor pressed Rylee's stomach against the wall, gripping her hands possessively. He nipped her neck. "I want you, darling," he said as her breath quickened and her body rubbed against his. He slipped his hands under her shirt, unsnapped her bra, slid it off, and squeezed her nipples. She groaned, arching her back like Clover did when being pet.

Connor spun her around so that she faced him, undid the buttons, and removed the blouse. Her breasts, now loose, were magnificent. Rylee didn't hide her body from him anymore. He took hold of the waistband of her skirt and panties and brought them down to her ankles together. He stood back up and offered his hand, helping her remove her clothing, then placed her up against the wall again. She was like the women in a Renoir painting, her body round and pink, made for frolicking and fucking. Someday soon, he'd fill their bed with flowers before bedding her, just like the painting.

"You're beautiful, love," he said as he cradled her head, kissing her. He brought his lips to her nipples, sucking. He dragged his teeth across them, leaving marks, then nibbled on them.

She sighed and moaned. "Keep going," she said.

Connor brought his fingers to her pussy to test her willingness, sliding two of them in quickly. She whimpered as he brought them out. He didn't want her empty, so he pushed them in again, dragging them across her clit and then making the return trip to her pussy, as she tried to clench down and capture them.

"You want this, then?" Connor whispered in her ear, taking his tongue and swirling it in her ear canal. She shivered and stretched her neck, opening herself to him. He licked her neck and left little bite marks over it. Rylee reached down and grabbed his cock, still tucked in his pants, making him throb and grow larger. "Behave or face the consequences," he said.

"Connor, please. No torture today," she begged.

"Pleasure and pain go together, and it always ends with pleasure. It's good for you to wait for your orgasm. We don't want things to end too quickly," he said, stopping and removing his cock from his pants. "Now that you've woken Master Goodfellow, you'll have to deal with him."

\* \* \*

CJ picked up her hand and wrapped it around his enlarged cock. She moved her hand to the tip, picking up pre-cum and spreading it down the length of his cock. He grabbed her ass, spreading her butt cheeks and dipping the top of his moist finger into her anus, teasing her and pushing in deeper with every stroke. "I need your tight little ass wrapped around my cock today. Are you down with that, my pretty?" She'd never enjoyed anal play—it was something her ex made her do—but CJ did it differently. Calm, tender. He knew how to get her worked up enough to beg for his cock in her ass, to own every part of her body.

"Get up here. I need to eat you." CJ pointed to the old wooden kitchen table. He planted his hands on her waist and helped her lift her ass up. "Lay back, lovely." She lay with her legs bent and spread open. Connor stood at the end of the table, seeing all of her, his eyes admiring. He makes her feel good about her body, not ashamed. *I'm more than good enough.*

CJ pulled up a chair and sat down like he was at a dinner party. He rolled the sleeves of his white shirt up, dragged his fingers up her thighs and down again, and parted the folds around her clitoris. "So pretty," he murmured, then brought his face to her pussy and began licking her, sucking and pulling. *I'm close already. There's no way to hide it from CJ. He knows every part of me and which buttons to push.* He didn't let her come. It was always like that—he wanted her to beg him for it, keeping her on edge for as long as he could, and he was great at it. He knew a little something about torture and pleasure.

He brought one of his fingers to her pussy and inserted it just a little, bringing it out again, teasing her, making her want more, while he continued to suck on her clit. "Please, CJ..." she moaned, grasping the back of his head. "Please make me cum."

"Not yet," he said, lifting his head. "Not until I give you permission." He kept bringing her close to climax and then stopping, close and then stopping, until she was writhing all over the table and he had to put one arm on her to hold her down.

"If you keep doing that, I'm going to cum no matter how hard I try not to," she said.

He stopped. "If you do, you're a bad girl, and you know what happens to bad girls. I make them start from the beginning again."

"Oh no," she said, smiling.

"Come down here, lovely. Give me your pretty ass." She got down from the table, desperate for release, her face blushing, getting on her hands and knees on the floor, putting her ass in the air and waiting for him. She looked behind her and watched as CJ approached.

His eyes growing huge, he fell to his knees and ran his hand between her legs, bringing it up to her drenched pussy and then past it to her ass. "You're good and wet, but I have our little friend to make things even easier for my lovely." He reached into his pocket and brought out the silver aluminum dildo that had recently become her dearest friend. He had purchased a set of various sizes, and they were finally up to the largest. "You've come a long way," he said, working the dildo into her ass. Her body tensed and she felt her anus trying to squeeze the dildo out. "Relax and breathe," he whispered into her ear. "Don't fight it. I won't push until you're ready." He held it where it was while he went back to her clit with his other hand, moistening her even more and making her need to be filled excruciating. "Now play with it yourself."

She pushed her fingers underneath his hand and started rubbing herself. CJ grabbed the end of the silver dildo and slid it in further, until it popped all the way inside her effortlessly. "There we go. Your ass wanted this." After a minute or two, he pulled the silver bullet out. He then pushed it in again, fucking her ass with the dildo, her body accepting it, aching for it as she played with her clit. Her temperature rose, her face and chest becoming flushed, and she couldn't help but start panting. "Not yet, my pretty," he said in a ragged voice. "Hold out another minute."

But Rylee wasn't sure she could hold out much longer. She moved her entire body with the dildo's thrusts, desperate for release. "I'm finally ready, CJ. I need you in my ass."

"You're sure about this? You think you can take all of me?"

She didn't know if she could or not, but she was so worked up at this point. "Fuck me in the ass, CJ. Please. Please fuck me in the ass."

CJ now straddled her, one arm around her waist to keep her pinned to him. He took his other hand and removed the dildo, little by little. He placed it on the floor next to them and brought the head of his cock up to her anus, teasing and testing her. She pressed back, trying to drive him in. CJ laughed. "You don't know what you're asking for. You've made me very large, woman. Best to let me drive." He suddenly pushed the tip of his wet dick in, stretching her anus, the pain beginning.

CJ hadn't lied. His dick was huge, like a hot wet poker being shoved in her ass. She resisted it at first, her ass clenching and her breathing uneven. He took another toy out of his pocket, but she couldn't see it. She only felt the vibrations as he brought it to her pussy and slid it in. It felt good to have her cunt filled with the large vibrating dildo. The humming radiated inside her, and that pleasure and her own fingers rubbing on her clit overrode the pain from CJ pushing into her ass. She exhaled and inhaled again until her breathing became even.

He pushed a little more into her with each thrust, bit by bit. "You're such a good girl," he groaned into her ear from behind, his own breath now becoming ragged too. He had reached the end of himself now, and her ass was entirely full with his cock. He spun up the speed of the dildo inside her cunt, distracting her. Her ass was now fully contracted around him, the pain gone and her pleasure blooming. He was now able to fully slide his cock in and out fast and hard, his balls slapping against her lips with each thrust. There was no holding him back now, her body no longer fighting him. CJ moved in and out faster and harder while he turned down the speed and power on the vibrator in her pussy, building up her desire and need. He roughly pushed her hand away from her clit and took over himself, expertly separating her lips with two fingers and rubbing her clit with a third. He pounded his cock into her ass, and she answered his thrusts with her own.

"I'm ready, my darling," he moaned into her ear. "Cum for me now." Sobs broke out of her. She felt her orgasm starting deep in her belly and shooting rapidly to her clit. Her ass tightened around his cock, the bars from his piercings hitting the sides of her anus as he thrust in and out. Her pussy clenched down on the dildo and waves of pleasure ripped through her, making her legs buckle and her body blend with the floor. CJ cried out, too: "I'm not done with you yet!" Pushing his body heavily onto her prone figure on the floor, he grabbed onto her hair with one hand, continuing to fuck her ass, searching for release. She stayed with him as he climaxed and spilled his fire into her, his face contorted into a sexy monster she can never get enough of. She felt powerful under him as they united in their shared pleasure and exhaustion.

"Was that good for you?" CJ asked a minute later, gingerly pulling himself from her ass and taking the vibrator out of her pussy.

"Couldn't you tell?" she asked, laughing. She turned over and took her place inside his arms as they laid on the floor together. Suddenly she began blinking. "Oh, shit, I lost a contact lens."

"I must have fucked it out of you," he laughed, losing his hands in her hair and stroking her head.

*Ring. Ring.* Rylee's phone. "I can call them back later," she told him, but he reached for her skirt on the floor with his foot and dragged it to them. CJ brought his hand to her breasts and played with her nipples as she answered it, licking and sucking as she tried not to scream out.

"Hi, Eric." Pause. "Another one? Really? I never expected

that." Pause. "Ouch!" Pause. "No, a bee stung me, I think. No worries."

CJ licked her belly button, picked up the vibrator, and turned it on, bringing it to her clit. She mouthed *no* while playfully slapping him, but he continued. "You think so? Call me Friday, let me know how it goes. Look, sorry, gotta run." She pressed the "end call" button and threw her phone down.

"*Hitman's Honey*?" CJ asked, temporarily lifting his mouth from her breast and the vibrator from her clit.

"There's a bidding war. Three publishers are fighting over it."

"Of course they are, it's going to be a hit," CJ said, holding the vibrator like a gun and winking. Then he went back to work on her.

Rylee collapsed into a puddle of pleasure, closing her eyes and giving a wild grin. "Oh, *CJaaaaaaaaaay!*"

## The End

Thank you for reading! Please rate this book!

# Also by Kay Freeman

Book 1 The Devil You Know, The Devil Chronicle Series

Book 2 Leather Man

Book 3 The Devil I Love, The Devil Chronicle Series

Find wherever you purchase your books!

# About the Author

Kay Freeman spent the early part of her career as a professional artist. She's shown her work throughout the United States under her professional name, Kay A. Klotzbach. She was awarded two Geraldine Dodge fellowships for her paintings from the State of New Jersey. Kay was a full-time art professor in South Jersey for over twenty-three years and was granted a Princeton Mid-Career Fellowship for her teaching and her community based learning projects.

Kay decided to pursue her passion for writing after her manuscript, *Truth Moon,* was selected by Romance Writers of America's RAMP program in 2021, which led to the publication of her debut novel, *Truth Moon,* by The Wild Rose Press. Kay has gone on to self-publish four other novels. She also writes a publication for romance authors, *What Do Romance Authors Think About,* a free newsletter on Substack.

Freeman is passionate about contemporary gothic and suspense romance. Kay loves to balance dark characters with more spiritual ones when writing her novels, providing ways for heroes and heroines to transform themselves into better people. Besides her passion for art, reading, and writing, she loves the blues, tequila, her husband Barry, and her standard poodle, Tango. This list is not intended to be in any particular order. Kay lives in Wilmington, DE, in a mid-century, modern kit home designed by Donald Scholz that she and her husband are still in the process of restoring.

You can reach Kay at KaylaaFreeman.com

www.ingramcontent.com/pod-product-compliance
Lightning Source LLC
Chambersburg PA
CBHW051251170626
46809CB00004B/1590